KIDNAP
TRUMP

by
DAVID CUNLIFFE

Grosvenor House
Publishing Limited

This book is published by
Grosvenor House Publishing Ltd
Link House
140 The Broadway, Tolworth, Surrey, KT6 7HT.
www.grosvenorhousepublishing.co.uk

A CIP record for this book
is available from the British Library

ISBN 978-1-78623-609-8

To my late Father Leslie Cunliffe
who loved reading Action Thrillers.

The year is two thousand and fifteen, a boy with amazing powers sits on a bed in a small dwelling on the edge of the Latin quarter of Paris. He is fifteen years of age and his name is David.

He sits lost in a world of his own, he picks out cards from a deck at random. A draught of cold air suddenly ran down his spine as he picked out the ace of spades. He then slipped into a deep trance, picking out three kings his abilities are remarkable.

He is of average build and has a gleaming face with very pale skin. All of a sudden, the door creaks open It was his father Gerald, a scientist a bearded man complete with a face of cool ivory. He looks to his son and smiles he then spoke, "in a low voice, "Hi, David have you had any more visions of future events?" David's ice blue eyes flickered and then he looked up to his Father with a fixed expression and replied, "Yes Father, I dreamt of a helicopter crash, it was navy blue in colour I watched as it lost control and crashed into a field and then it exploded into flames, I don't think there were any survivors, I believe five people including the pilot all perished in the accident."

Gerald's eyes perked with curiosity he knew his son had made correct predictions in the past. He reached inside his pocket; he then produced a mobile phone with great speed he checked the latest news. A picture appeared a navy-blue helicopter crashed into a deserted field. Gerald was shocked to hear the news that the five people in the helicopter including the pilot all died instantly.

Gerald then turned to his son and said, "David, do you know what caused the crash?" David looked up at his father with sorrow filling his warm heart he replied, "Father it was the motor, it just packed in and then the pilot lost control, they had no chance."

His father was middle-aged, well-groomed and he wore a white shirt and dark trousers. Gerald had been conducting experiments in the field of extrasensory perception for many years, he spent all of his time devoted to testing his son's special powers. Gerald placed his phone back into his pocket he then smiled at David and said, "Alright son, are you ready for some more tests today? You are to be filmed in the laboratory, the Government shall know of your special powers, maybe in the future, they could be put to some good use."

David stood up nodding his head in agreement, he placed his pack of cards under his pillow next to his favourite book entitled "Nostradamus visions of future events". Gerald left the room as David quickly opened up his wardrobe and then got out his favourite clothes, he walked over to the bathroom a quick wash, he then brushed his teeth and got dressed in a blue polo neck shirt and matching blue pants. David looked into the mirror, brushing his golden hair, a cheeky smile, then he was on his way downstairs.

His father sat in the dining room drinking strong coffee. David entered the room, his Father pointed to the table he had prepared a quick breakfast for him, David sat down and began to eat his breakfast. Gerald laughed and said, "I see you are all dressed up in your favourite colour, my little boy blue." David sat eating his breakfast he began to yawn, ignoring his Fathers comments.

David soon finished his breakfast, one last drink of his pure orange juice, he then stood up and announced he had finished. Gerald smiled and said, "Alright son let's go." David agreed and followed his Father outside to the red car parked on the driveway. David closed the front door behind him and then walked over to the car. The door was open, he climbed in and then closed the door.

Gerald then drove towards the lab; the radiant glory of the sun was so bright David shaded his eyes. As they drove towards the lab a cool breeze slowly swept the silver trees that Napoleon had ordered planted in the seventeenth century.

The city of Paris was in all of its glory, the roads were busy, David could hear the sounds of disrupted drivers, the noise echoed all around, David closed his eyes. He craved solitude and peace, the car suddenly came to a halt and then a domineering voice echoed around the car "David are you asleep? wake up, we have arrived at the lab."

David opened his eyes his moment of peace was shattered, his eyes flickered for a brief second. Gerald spoke, "to his son with a voice of concern, "David are you alright?" David replied, "Yes Father I was just resting my eyes for a second." Gerald then said, "Alright son, it doesn't matter, as long as you feel alright, remember there will be an observer who works for the Government making notes and you are to be filmed for the first time, make sure you smile for the camera, just be yourself."

David was lost for words and just nodded his head. Gerald passed through security with David close by his side, he then swiped his card to the lab, the door quickly opened Gerald held the door open and they both entered. David looked at the security cameras, he blinked as the light caught his eyes. All of a sudden, a man appeared he spoke in a low voice, "Hello my name is Lucas I am the cameraman, everything is set up ready for the experiment."

Gerald then introduced David, "This is my son, David what about the government official has he arrived?" Lucas replied, "Yes Gerald, his name is Eric, shall we go and meet him?" Gerald replied, "Yes let's go."

Lucas had thick, black, curly hair, a tanned face, he wore baggy, faded jeans and a pale green top. Inside the far corner of the Lab sat a tall man in a dark tailored suit, he had tender looks with heavy dark eyebrows. He stood up and spoke, "with a voice of concern, "Hello my name is Eric." He moved forward taking big strides, he stretched out his hand and greeted Gerald with a warm handshake. Eric then turned his attention to David and said, "This must be the star of the show I have heard all about psychic powers, fame and fortune await you, my friend."

Gerald then spoke out in a rage, "My son is here for the good of France, not fame and fortune." Frowning in confusion Eric spoke back with firmness in his voice, "You are right, you accept my apologies." Gerald acknowledged his words, he then looked down at David and said, "My son, this is your hour, I want you to show them what you can do." Eric returned to his seat, he opened a briefcase and removed a laptop from it ready to record the results of the experiment.

Lucas stood next to the camera ready to film the experiment David sat in his usual seat, his heart was pounding, panic fears fluttered his mind. David then heard a voice, he then regained his composure, his Father said, "David keep cool, let us begin first with the shapes." Lucas began to film the experiment; he loved his work as a cameraman.

Gerald asked for Eric's assistance, "My friend, could you please go behind the screen over there and place shapes into the small empty containers and then seal the lids, and then the first test will begin." Eric nodded in approval, he walked over to the back of the screen and then proceeded to place various shapes into boxes, Gerald called out to Eric, "Have you completed the task?" Eric appeared with the sealed containers stacked on top of a tray, Gerald smiled and said, "Good, you have the right idea, now bring the tray over and place it in front of my son."

Gerald picked up a blindfold, he placed it over his son's eyes he then spoke in a deep voice, "Right Eric, you have placed five shapes into five containers and sealed the lids, I will now open one of the containers, we shall demonstrate the use of communication between minds."

Gerald removed the lids of the first container and then concentrated on the shape. "Right David what shape is it?" David without hesitation informed his Father, "It is a triangle." "Correct, right the next container." Gerald removed the lid and concentrated on the shape. "Number two is a hexagon." "Correct, right the third container." David concentrated, a second later he spoke, "with confidence, "The next shape is a square." Before Gerald could open the lid, David informed his father that the next shape was an octagon. Eric stood amazed with eyes as wide as the ocean. Gerald then said, "Alright you are too good, what is the last shape?" David sat motionless and then without warning he spoke, "The final shape is a hexagon."

Gerald smiled he then spoke, "in a heightened voice, "Right Eric you may remove the lid." Eric hesitated and then removed the lid to reveal a hexagon, he then turned to Gerald and said, "My you are gifted." Gerald agreed and then slowly removed his son's blindfold. He then said, "Now for the next test are you ready son?" David nodded his head.

Gerald then produced a compass from his pocket he then placed it on the table in front of his son. Eric picked up the compass and after a close examination placed it back on the table next to David. Gerald smiled once more he then whispered, "My son you know what to do next let us all see the compass needle move, use the power of your mind." David concentrated and within minutes the compass needle began to move, Gerald moved various scientific instruments beside David, he placed electrodes on his head and then carried on with the experiment.

David continued to make the needle move, Eric looked at the scientific equipment, the readings where amazing, the needle began to move faster and faster, Gerald spoke in a heightened voice, "My son is now generating tremendous energy, can you not feel the power?"

The needle was now turning at great speed. "That is enough proof." all of a sudden, the needle stopped rotating Gerald removed the compass placing it in his pocket, he then turned to Eric and said, "Ok Eric how are you when it comes to drawing?" Eric laughed out loud, admitting it was not one of his best skills. Gerald reflected a shade of disappointment and said, "Never mind Eric, just try your best, I want you to sit behind the screen, there you will find pencils and paper I want you to draw an object, after that I want you to place the paper inside your pocket return and concentrate on the object you have just drawn." Eric agreed, and then sat behind the screen, he drew a picture of his cat sitting gazing out of a window this was a picture of his pet cat he had named Paris. He quickly folded the piece of paper and placed it inside his pocket, he then returned from behind the screen. Eric stood before David and pictured his cat sitting in the window at home. Gerald turned to David and said, "Right my son what can you see?" David replied with a firmness in his voice, "I see a strange-looking cat in Paris gazing out of a window, the pet cat you named Paris." Eric began to frown in confusion with an expression of horror he spoke, "We have never met, it is impossible for you to know the name of my cat or to know it likes to sit in my window, you, my friend are truly amazing."

Eric then produced the picture as the cameraman zoomed in. Gerald laughed and the said, "Okay Eric for the next test I want you to return behind the screen, I want you to draw a scene from your early years a secret only you know about." Eric agreed and said, "Alright I won't be needing this." Eric handed the picture to Gerald who placed it next to David. He then smiled and said, "You were correct it is indeed a strange-looking cat."

Eric shook his head then returned behind the screen. He sat as childhood memories flashed before him, he then picked up a pencil and began to draw a packet of cigarettes, a local shop and the Police. Once again, he folded the piece of paper and then placed it into his pocket. Eric then returned from behind the screen, he then announced that it was impossible for David to know a dark secret of his past, not even his wife or family knew about. Eric had one problem he was so confident he had forgotten he was being filmed.

Gerald in a confident voice said, "Ok we shall see Eric think about what happened all of those years ago." David shook his head and began to laugh out loud, "No wonder it's a secret, after all, you are a Government officer, you were caught stealing cigarettes for your friends from a local shop, you were arrested, but your father put in a good word and you were let off with a telling off."

Eric shook his head and produced the piece of paper placing it on the table next to David, he then spoke in a confused voice, "All of this is too much information and to think I am being filmed I have to say I have read your reports on your son, he can speak Latin and four different languages, he has the power to predict future events, he is very special and we all have a moral responsibility to make sure his gift is used for the good of our great nation."

Eric smiled, he then talked fluently in a heightened voice, "I am very patriotic, I will now go away and make out my report, my superiors will read my report and view these remarkable experiments."

Eric shook hands with Gerald and David, he then collected his laptop and left. As Lucas packed up his camera and equipment Gerald smiled at Lucas and said, "It has been a pleasure to have you here filming these experiments." Lucas replied, "Your son, David was like a shining star." Gerald agreed. He then spoke to David, "Are you hungry?" David nodded his head and replied, "Yes." Gerald laughed and said, "Okay the star of the show is hungry it's time to go."

All three began to laugh out loud and then slowly left the room. Gerald held the door open as Lucas departed. Gerald then turned to David, he embraced him and said, "Well done son, you were sensational." David smiled as they both walked over to the parked-up Citroen automobile, they both got in. Gerald then drove towards home, the radiant glory of the sun shone down. The traffic was now frantic, the echo of car horns rang out in Gerald's ears, he tried to keep his cool, but anxiety twisted his face. He then expressed his annoyance he shouted, "Bloody tourists!" A pigeon then flew into his windscreen, Gerald screamed at the bird as it deposited a large white mark on his windscreen, it then regained its composure and flew off into the sky. Gerald shook his head and shouted, "Bloody pigeons they're everywhere!"

David just sat with his eyes closed, he often had visions of a place with an atmosphere of peace and tranquillity, his Father finally regained his composure and they continued the journey in silence. David listened to the sound of the windscreen wipers disposing of the mess the pigeon had deposited.

They soon arrived home and then a familiar voice, David's eyes remained closed Gerald spoke in a deep voice, "David are you asleep? Have you tired after all those experiments?" David opened his eyes slowly, he then replied, "Yes, I do feel a bit tired." Gerald then said, "Okay let's get inside its food and a drink that's what you need." David agreed, and they both got out of the car and then entered their dwelling.

Inside they were both greeted by Christina, she had a such a warm smile, a tall slim brunette dressed in a green silk dress complete with freshness and grace, her eyes of emerald green were so engaging. She was a very kind-hearted woman of confidence and compassion. Gerald embraced his wife, he kissed her passionately on her ruby red lips as David sat down at the table.

Everything was set, complete with a freshly cut baguette. Christina enquired about the experiments, Gerald smiled and said, "It was all a complete success." She then entered the kitchen and after a few minutes, she returned with a tray, on the tray three bowls of French soup. Gerald quickly sat down, as this was his favourite soup. He looked to Christina and spoke in a loud voice, "I love the smell of onions." Gerald reached for a glass of white wine, he took a slow sip, Christina lit a candle on the table as David looked on mesmerized by the flame.

Gerald gazed at his son and said, "David are you alright?" David replied in a low voice, "Yes Father." Gerald shook his head and spoke, "Sometimes you look so distant in a world of your own." Christina disagreed and spoke to Gerald with a raised voice, "Leave him alone, it's all of these experiments the poor boy must be tired." Gerald nodded his head, he then apologised to David.

All of the food was soon gone, David looked to his father, he yawned then spoke with a tired voice, "Is it right if I go to my room and read?" Gerald laughed and replied, "Let me guess you require enlightenment it's a book about Nostradamus." David nodded and said, "yes, "He made some truly amazing predictions." Gerald agreed as David got up and made his way to his bedroom.

Christina laughed as she poured out more wine into her glass she then said, "Wherever does he get his intellect from?" Gerald embraced his wife smiling from ear to ear, he then replied, "Why me, of course." Christina pushed Gerald and they both begin to laugh out loud.

David stood in the corner of his bedroom, he picked out a book from a large bookshelf, it contained books of logic and all the various languages he had studied over the years, including Latin. His room was always tidy, his parents had taught him to respect his surroundings. He sat on his bed and opened it up and was soon engrossed in the life story of Nostradamus. Suddenly the weather changed, and the rain started to patter against his bedroom window followed by the howl of the wind.

The time flew by and soon he had finished reading, he began to feel drowsy he changed his clothes and was soon asleep in bed. All of a sudden, the bedroom door opened, it was his mother, Christina she looked down at him fast asleep, she smiled and then closed the door behind her.

David was in a deep sleep, he dreamt of Nostradamus and then found himself following a ray of light, it produced such a deep fascination David felt at peace as he followed a bright light along a golden tunnel. Very soon he departed from the tunnel into a different dimension, he looked to his feet beneath them was pure white sand, he scanned all around them drew a deep breath, he rubbed his eyes as they began to flicker. He then started walking towards a figure in the distance, the atmosphere was warm he looked up at the stars, they shone bright with wrath.

David began to move faster and faster, curiosity was his inspiration, a draught of cold air suddenly ran down his spine, he proceeded with great caution. After a short walk, he found he had reached his destination, glowing with anticipation he looked to a mysterious figure. David gazed and then reflected a shade of terror, a strange creature stood before him dressed in a golden robe. The creature spoke in a deep voice, "Welcome to my domain young David Trump, my name is Cavoc the ruler of the fifth dimension."

David gazed spellbound into Cavoc's bright emerald eyes. He then spoke once more in a deep confident voice, "You are but a mere child, my sight must be so frightening to one so young, please do not let your mind be paralysed by my hideous sight, speak, that is why you are here, you possess extraordinary powers. I believe you are of the same bloodline as another David who visited me here in the fifteenth century, assisted by Nostradamus, his name was David Burns. He had such an unhappy ending at the hands of Mabus. David was torched and burnt at the stake."

David had read in his book about Mabus, Nostradamus had written Mabus was pure evil. Cavoc's words rolled around in his head, he began frowning in confusion. David then said, "Tell me more who David Burns was."

Cavoc laughed out loud and then spoke, "Well you are such refreshing company, you have a tongue you can speak, right let me enlighten you. David Burns travelled from England, his mission was to visit me and help create the wealth of which I needed, I gave him a book with the formula to transmute lead into gold which you will agree was a sound investment. I believe the price of gold in your dimension continues to rise, I wanted to meet in the land of dreams as we are now. Nostradamus played his part, his reward for helping me, the book you have read several times. His predictions of the future, in reality, I made the predictions, he listened and altered them into verses. Back in the fifteenth century, good and evil crossed over to your domain from my dimension at will, so much violation, but all of this had to come to an end. Mankind evolved weapons of mass destruction. Very soon mankind's judgement day will be here, it is but ten years away. Anyway back to David Burns, he founded the

Five Fives to keep the balance in my dimension every twenty-five years, five chosen gifted individuals have crossed over to the Fifth dimension and done battle for riches beyond their comprehension, the last was how strange, the day you were born, in the year two thousand the Millennium. If only I had the power to turn back the clock, but time is everyone's worst enemy, you cannot compete for when you are twenty-five years of age your world will cease unless you have greater powers in time to change the future of mankind."

David listened to Cavoc's cold words and then abruptly interrupted Cavoc, "How will the world end?" Cavoc shook his head and replied, "Patience young man, listen I have so much to tell you, conversation is what I crave, knowledge is but a seed which grows and grows, Right, let me tell you all about the end of the world. There are five possible endings, I cannot predict which one will destroy mankind.

The first is China, without warning it will destroy the New World, China has many allies that will take over Europe. After the death of the New world an almighty war will engulf all until the world is destroyed, the next possible ending is an alien invasion without mercy mankind will be wiped out, the next a virus a superbug that will spread like wildfire with no cure, man will fall at death's door, and then we have the collapse of the ozone layer due to global warming, mankind suffers a slow agonising death, the final of the five is a giant comet the destruction of the earth will be swift that is all five China , Alien, Virus ,Ozone and Comet. Yes, I know you are well educated, the first five letters spell out my name, Cavoc.

Back to your world, it revolves around wealth nothing can be obtained without wealth, David Burns helped me obtain vast amounts of wealth for my future plans, for that I was truly grateful. He was betrayed by Mabus who served a demonic master who was reborn as a mass murderer. You will know him as Hitler."

David listened mesmerised by the dark unfolding story, "All of this, believe it or not, started off in Roman times, a Jew by the name of Cabol produced a steady supply of gold, he transformed lead to gold from an old book. I stole the book and brought it back with me to the fifth dimension. A demonic Roman reaped his wrath against the Jews until they finally killed him, unfortunately for mankind, he was reborn again in the nineteenth century and exacted revenge on the Jewish population. He created camps of mass extermination and slaughtered millions of Jews. Imagine if good had not defeated evil I believe you would not be standing before me now. He occupied Paris when the allies arrived in France, he ordered his troops to kill and destroy, this order was not completed and here you stand.

The war lasted six years, there were six million Jews murdered altogether sixty million died, the mark of the beast. David, you must be wondering, is this but a dream maybe a nightmare? I am but a figment of your wondering wild imagination, believe me, I am quite real.

Your surname Trump, a French surname introduced to England in 1066 by the Norman invaders. In 2016 the surname Trump will ring out all over the World, for he will be elected as the President of the New World. This man is like a coin he has two sides one quite brilliant and another quite paranoid, he believes the Chinese invented Global warming to attack New world manufacturing, he surrounds himself with people who feed him the wrong advice. Global warming due to Trump backing the dirty- energy industry, there will be catastrophic and irreversible consequences for humanity on your Planet. Oh, and by the way David my friend, you are in great danger your father, Gerald has made a grave error, the experiments filmed in his laboratory will fall into the wrong hands, men from the New world will witness your remarkable abilities and see it as a way of making riches beyond their wildest dreams."

David summed up the courage to speak in a low voice, he spoke, "What must I do for the best?" Cavoc shook his head and said, "nothing. Whenever I predict the future there is no changing it." David spoke once more, "Cavoc, is mankind doomed to destruction in the year two thousand and twenty-five?"

Cavoc looked down at David's concerned face and spoke, "I am afraid so." "Is there anything I can do to change the outcome?" Cavoc replied, "Just imagine, David the year 2025 and your planet, Earth with a lifeline of twenty-five years taking it to the year 2050 would that not be amazing. Let me consult Numerology, the numbers never lie. The number two represents the letter B, the number five is E, add two and five together and you are left with the number seven, so we have G. This spell out a word, not a very nice word if you want your World to last beyond 2025 you must beg. David your time is up, you must go now, remember the men from the New World will come and visit you, Saint Francis will help you, good will conquer over evil."

David gazed into Cavoc's eyes and then spoke in his low voice, "Thank you, Cavoc, will our paths ever cross again?" Cavoc smiled and replied, "Maybe, if so by some miracle your world does not end then we will meet again as I believe you will be one of the five competing for the ultimate prize. I hope our conversation has enlightened you." David smiled, he said, " goodbye to Cavoc, he then turned and walked back towards the tunnel and then a familiar voice, ", it was his mother, Christina, she spoke in a quiet voice, "Wake up David, wake up or you will be late for school."

David collected his thoughts, the New world Cavoc mentioned, he must have been talking about America. The results of the experiment had spread across the world with the aid of the internet.

In Washington DC, Agents Harry and Ryan were summoned to their chief's headquarters, they were a couple of old school C.I.A. agents assigned to overseas cases, observing and reporting their findings. Harry, a real rough, solidly built complete with moustache, heavy suntanned and dark sunglasses. His partner, Ryan, a younger tall blonde haired, thin figure complete with designer shades, both dressed in dark tailored suits.

They pulled up in a dark coloured Cadillac, Harry looked in his mirror, well-groomed as usual, he then looked to his partner and said, "Overseas assignment you reckon?" Ryan was tall and deep-voice, "d he replied, "Yes I reckon, let's get to her office and find out, the suspense is killing me."

Harry opened the door to his Cadillac, Ryan followed suit. The sun shone in all its glory, they both made their way past security and then a short journey through one building, and then into the chief's office, a knock on the door a brief delay and then they both entered the office.

Chief Mellor sat awaiting their company, he was larger than life, a shrivelled complexion and death cold eyes, a giant imposing man complete with grey sideburns, an African American and proud of the fact. He was sweating furiously; he then reached over and turned his desk fan to the maximum.

He looked at Harry the Ryan and began to speak, "Ok you guys, grab a seat I have an assignment for you." Harry and Ryan sat down as the chief continued to speak fluently with a heightened voice, "My superiors are concerned about some experiments that were conducted on a fifteen-year-old boy in Paris, he was studied and investigated by an independent observer. I have watched the film and read the report, this young guy believe you me, is remarkable. He has amazing powers, various departments want you pair to go over and have a chat with his parents, maybe they could relocate to our fair City."

Ryan sniggers, a wide grin took over his face. Chief Mellor shook his head and then spoke in a deep voice, "Look Ryan don't piss me off, this city pays your wages and don't you forget that or I'll have you busted down to a beat Cop in the suburbs, how would you like that?"

Ryan looked down and mumbled, "Sorry Chief I wouldn't like that." Chief Mellor laughed and said, "Yes well just concentrate on what I am saying, just listen, the boy is fifteen, his name is David Trump, his Father Gerald a scientist and his mother is called Christina. I know what you're thinking Harry, the cold war is over, but news of this kid is spreading fast, imagine the Chinese and Russians might be sending agents to Paris as we speak."

Harry looked into Mellor's eyes and said, "Ok is this kid related to Donald Trump, the big guy who owns the towers?" Chief Mellor shook his head, and then Harry continued talking, "So when do you want to leave for Paris?" the Chief replied, "Now, straight away, here is the envelope."

Mellor handed Harry a large brown, "Inside the envelope is your tickets and a briefing on what to do when you arrive in Paris, I presume you both have your passports ready at hand." Harry looked at Ryan and said, "I've mine you got yours?" Ryan smiled and replied, "Yes here in my jacket pocket, looks like we are going to Paris." Chief Mellor looked to Harry and said, "No fuck-ups, I want this operation to run smoothly understand?" Harry nodded his head in agreement and replied, "Yes Chief, you can trust us have we ever let you down?"

Chief Mellor shook his head and then replied, "in a raised voice, "Alright you couple of smart asses, if it makes you feel any better, we are desperate, we had no one else available now get the hell out of here." Harry shook his head and collected the brown envelope and then they both stood up and left the building and proceeded towards their car.

Harry handed the brown envelope to Ryan and said, "Right do something useful read what mad Mellor has written." Ryan replied, "Alright." as he and Harry got into the car Ryan pulled out a classified file, he started to read out loud as Harry started up the car and pulled away towards Ronald Reagan airport. A brief silence and then hysterical laughter, Harry became angry and said, "Look, Ryan, tell me what's so Goddamn funny, read out the report."

Ryan smiled and replied, "Yeah okay Harry." He then read out the report. "They are investigating the possibility of using paranormal powers such as telepathy for intelligence gathering purposes, anyone demonstrating a high level of special powers, psychic abilities must be seized upon and exploited for the good of our proud nation. What a load of crap, another mad Mellor mission do you believe in all that crap?"

Harry turned to Ryan and replied, "We get paid to believe in any crap they throw at us, you heard Chief Mellor, one thing I do believe they wouldn't be sending us all the way to Paris at the expense of the taxpayers if they didn't believe in this kid's abilities. I want you to just sit there and think about it." A brief delay and Ryan spoke in an enlightened voice, "My God! You're right as usual."

Harry nodded his head and then accelerated. As the sun continued to beat down on them, Harry began to sweat ferociously, the traffic became more and more congested suddenly his anger erupted like a volcano, followed by a sinister expression, Ryan looked to Harry and said, "My, you look pissed off, I know this is an emergency ain't it." Harry forced a smile and said, "You're right it is."

All of a sudden Ryan's window opened, a siren was placed on the top of the car and that was Harry's ticket to speed past all the traffic, with an edge of coldness Harry weaved in and out of the traffic faster and faster until they arrived at the airport, parking in an underground car park. The siren was now off, silence at last.

Harry sank into his chair and collected his thoughts, Ryan turned to Harry and said, "The Plane leaves in one hour, what we need is a couple of Jack Daniel's." Harry agreed. He then parked his car in the car park, Ryan then said, "First things first, I need a cigarette, you are having one?" Harry replied, "Alright open the door first and pass me the brown envelope."

Ryan lit up a cigarette he handed one to Harry. Whilst Harry read the file on David, they smoked their cigarettes, Ryan looked to Harry and said, "What you reckon then Harry, is this kid the genuine article?" Harry replied, "You mean is he the one? I believe so, the key is his parents, remember I do all the talking understood?" Ryan replied, "as always Harry you do all the work, I am just here for the ride let's go and get ourselves a drink."

Harry and Ryan got out of the car, Harry opened the boot, inside sat two light travel prepacked bags. Harry handed Ryan his bag and then he locked up his car, slamming the boot behind him. They then proceed towards the lift Terminal Three. Harry pressed the button they entered the lift a sliding door closed quickly behind them, a press of the button and they are on their way.

Very soon the door opened, and they walked to a bar on Terminal Three, the airport is busy. Harry and Ryan informed Airport Security who they were, they then were escorted past the queue, they opened up their passports. Harry then said, "Secret Government business." He then produced the Aeroplane tickets, the Airport security officer scanned them then said, "Okay you guys have a nice day." Harry nodded in agreement, they then both walked towards the bar, Ryan checked out a group of female tourists, he said, "Hi Ladies." A beautiful blonde smiled, Harry turned his head, he focused on his partner and shouted, "Come on Ryan we haven't got time for this." Ryan smiled and then said,

"See you, ladies, again sometime." Harry shook his head with annoyance as Ryan rejoined him.

Ryan looked over to a bar and then spoke, "Look Harry over there a bar, it's Jack Daniel's time." Harry shook his head then spoke in a heightened voice, "Ok calm down you're like a kid in a candy shop." Harry walked up to the bar he looked to the barmaid and said, "Two Jack Daniel's on the rocks." She smiled and said, "Alright Sir, coming straight up very shortly."

The young barmaid returned with the drinks, she was pretty with pale skin and gleaming white teeth. Ryan looked into her eyes and said, "Haven't we met before?" Harry's patience was wearing thin, he turned to Ryan and said, "Knock it off Ryan we're here on business." Harry paid for the drinks and then they moved to a quiet section of the barroom, they both sat down with their drinks. Harry took a sip of his drink; he then vented his anger on Ryan "What's up with you? You're like a dog with two dicks ain't you are getting much at home?" Ryan shook his head and replied, "I am having a bit of fun, do you remember that concept? You're growing old Harry old misery guts."

Harry shook his head and said, "Less of the old I just want you to promise you're going to behave when we get to Paris." Ryan nodded his head in agreement and then said, "Alright Harry I promise from now on I will be on my best behaviour." Harry took another sip of his drink then spoke in a deep voice, "Good, drink up it's your round."

Harry and Ryan downed their drinks and then Ryan went to the bar. Whilst at the bar Ryan got out his mobile and sent a message to his wife, Cindy. Harry looked around the bar at various people drinking and laughing he thought to himself maybe I am getting too old for this job if only I had money, twenty years in this job and nothing to show for it.

Ryan returned with the drinks, he sat down and said, "You alright for a moment there you looked miles away I didn't upset you, did I?" Harry shook his head and replied in a low voice, "No you're right, twenty years, two failed marriages, all I have left is my pension and that is not much If only there was a way of making millions." Ryan replied, "I must admit Harry if I was given the opportunity to make millions, I would make it my own." Harry laughed and spoke, "You mean you would dissolve our partnership and look after number one?"

Ryan also laughed and replied, "Oh of course not Harry, fifty-fifty straight down the middle as, always right? Harry lets drink up and get on the plane for Paris." Harry agreed and they were both soon on a flight to France.

Back in Paris, David had just returned from school his mother answered the door with a warm smile she then said, "Hello David how was school?" David smiled and then entered following his mother to the kitchen. Christina was furiously sweating, it was such a hot day, she opened up the fridge and then poured orange juice into two glasses. Christina handed a drink to David he thanked her, Christina smiled and then spoke, "How did you sleep last night? I thought I heard you talking in your sleep."

David looked up to his Mother and spoke, "I had a strange dream, last night mum." Christina laughed and said, "Is it any wonder those books you are always reading some of them are a little strange." David laughed and said, "The dream, it was so vivid, I was pre-warned two men are coming for me from America, a creature from the fifth dimension told me his name is Cavoc, he also told me all about Hitler, did you know he was demonic? Also, the world will end in two thousand and twenty-Five." Christina shook her head then spoke in a heightened voice, "So much information for one dream and you remembered it all in so much detail that is amazing, such imagination. I want you to just forget about it let's talk about things closer to home, how is your friend Pepe? I remember you told me about his father, he lost his job." David remembered his promise and said, "They are to be thrown onto the street at the end of the month." Christina looked into David's eyes and then spoke in a firm voice, "You haven't said you would help them, have you?" David looked at Christina with a fixed expression and replied, "What possible harm could it do?" Christina began to look annoyed she replied, "David, I want to know everything."

David shook his head then said, "Well I told Pepe all about the psychic experiments, his family need money we both came up with a plan it's the euro millions, the jackpot is eighty million I have picked out the winning numbers." Suddenly her anger erupted like a volcano, "You fool I do not like what you have done, you're messing around with people's lives, giving them false hope, I have read in magazines people with psychic abilities have tried to predict the lottery since it began no one has achieved this as the odds are unbelievable."

David then took a deep breath and said, "Pepe and his father are calling around later and I am to give them the piece of paper with the numbers on it." Christina shook her head in disbelief she then spoke with anger in her voice, "Where is the piece of paper you have written on? Where is it?"

David looked up and replied, "Oh upstairs in my bedroom." Christina shook her head and spoke, "Go and get it now." His mother then followed him to his bedroom, in disbelief David entered his room he looked under his pillow inside his book of Nostradamus sat a piece of paper, David picked up the paper and then turned and handed it to his mother. Christina was still angry she gazed into David's eyes and said, "Right David I want you to stay in your room until your father returns home." David nodded his head and said, "But mother I was only trying to help Pepe and his poor family." Christina replied, "David don't you think I know that? But you must never change someone's destiny using your physic abilities."

David sat down on his bed in silence as his mother walked out of the bedroom. Very soon Gerald returned from work, he entered the house, he looked into Christina's eyes and automatically knew something was not right. He then said, "Christina what is the matter where is David?" Christina replied, "Oh I sent him to his room." Gerald shook his head and spoke in a confused voice, "Why?" Christina replied, "Remember I told you about his friend Pepe his father lost his job and they are to be evicted and thrown onto the street at the end of the month?" Gerald shook head and then spoke, "We are all sympathetic to their plight but what has that to do with David?"

Christina carried on with the story, "Well let me tell you he has told Pepe he will predict the winning numbers on the euro millions, thus they will live happily ever after, Pepe and his father are calling around later for the winning numbers written on this piece of paper."

A feeling of wild amazement engulfed his mind as Christina handed him the piece of paper, Gerald took hold of the piece of paper and said, "Did you know, Christina there is a rollover the jackpot is eighty million? All that money, the good we could do with it. Christina shook her head in disbelief and said, "Gerald do you really believe they are the winning numbers?" Gerald replied, "I honestly do not know what to believe."

Christina became angry and said, "Look, as I have explained to David his psychic powers must not be used to change people's destiny, no one should financially benefit from his gifts." Gerald said, "I am sorry Christina." He then placed the piece of paper into his trouser pocket, he then smiled and said, "Right now that is all sorted, I will go and have a word with our son whilst you fix us some dinner."

The CIA agents jet landed in Paris, Harry and Ryan slowly got off the jet they then walked through customs showing their passports and then proceeded out of the airport. Harry hailed a cab, the driver pulled over, Harry reached inside his pocket and handed the driver a card, on the card the name of a local hotel. He said, "Take me there, you understand?" The driver replied, "yes I understand, you are American yes?" Harry nodded and replied, "I am American." Ryan laughed and said, "It must be the accent hey Harry?" They both laughed as they got into the taxi with their bags.

The sky was now cloudy and overcast, the taxi driver was a bit of a slob, he had a shrivelled complexion complete with big bright brown eyes. Harry looked to Ryan and spoke in a low voice, "The word rancid springs to mind, why do all French people stink of garlic and onions?"

The driver looked at them in his mirror, Ryan laughed and said, "Hey Harry he must have heard you." Harry with a feeling of repulsion replied, "What is he going to do to me breathe on me?" And then hysterical laughter echoed around the taxi.

Shortly after that, the Taxi pulled over, they had arrived at their destination. Harry paid the Taxi driver, they then checked in and were soon outside the room. Harry opened the door and placed his bag next to a chair, Ryan entered gazing all around the room, he then made a comment, "Harry now this is what you call luxury." Harry shook his head and sat down on a chair. Ryan dropped his bag and then fell down backwards onto the nearest bed, Harry turned to Ryan and spoke, "It's communication time, me and you are going to have a wash, not together, I might add, and then we are going for a drink, and then onto their humble abode remember, let the cool guy do all the talking."

Ryan smiled and said, "My lips are forever sealed, you do all the talking that's fine by me Mr. cool guy." Harry laughed out loud.

Back in the Trump household, David lay on his bed lost in a daydream, all of a sudden, his mother entered the room and said, "Your dinner is now ready, come down me and your Father want another word with you." David climbed out of his bed and followed his mother to the dining area. There he sat down opposite his father. David closed his eyes for a brief second and then opened them and looked at his father steadily in the face.

Gerald thought for a moment and then spoke in a deep, gravelly voice, "Your mother has told me all about Pepe in great detail and how you wanted to help him, your heart is in the right place, not your head. I believe Pepe and his Father are coming around for the winning numbers they are expecting this piece of paper I have in my pocket what we both know it is impossible not even you could perform such a task."

David shook his head and then spoke, "I am so sorry, I felt so sorry for Pepe and his family." All of a sudden there was a knock on the door, David jumped to his feet, Gerald also stood up, he then told David to sit back down. "I shall deal with this." Christina looked to Gerald, she then spoke with a puzzled face, "Gerald what will you say?" Gerald replied, "Do not concern yourself, I know what to say."

Gerald walked over to the front door he heard another knock and slowly opened the door, standing on the doorstep was Pepe and his father, Charles who spoke in a deep voice, "Hello Gerald, can I speak with your son David?" Gerald shook his head and replied, "I am sorry, no you cannot, I know why you are here, me and my family offer you our deepest sympathy, David has amazing gifts, but he has a vivid imagination, did you honestly believe he could pick out the winning numbers on the euro millions?"

Pepe looked up to his father, Charles and said: "Father, Father he has shown me his special powers he can do it I know he can." A sense of doom engulfed Charles, he became angry and then spoke, with a raised voice, "Look, Gerald, your son promised Pepe the numbers let us have the numbers it has given my family great hope, what harm can it do? Let us at least put the numbers on and try."

Gerald was adamant he shook his head and spoke, in a deep voice, "No I am afraid not you would be wasting your money." Charles had massive biceps and bulged shoulders, his testosterone levels rose and rose, he then spoke, in an angry voice, "Gerald you are making me angry give me the numbers." Gerald remained calm and replied, "Sorry I cannot I must go now."

Gerald moved with great haste closing the front door behind him, several bangs on the front door then Gerald regained his composure, an anxious silence and then Christina appeared, she said, "Sorry I should have warned you Pepe's father is always pumped up with steroids, a complete meathead, not the sort of man you can reason with." Gerald smiled, he shrugged his shoulders and said, "You can say that again."

Christina had such an engaging smile; her features were delicately drawn such a comfort to the eye. They embraced, she stroked his hair and then passionately kissed him on the lips.

All of a sudden David appeared, he pointed to the smell in the kitchen and said, "What is that smell?" Christina grinned broadly and replied, "My god it's the dinner." She rushed into the kitchen turning off the oven with great haste. She opened the oven door, smoke from the overcooked lamb engulfed the kitchen. Christina began to curse as she placed the baking tray on top of the cooker.

Gerald looked into Christina's eyes and said, "Is there anything I can do?" Christina nodded and said,

"Yes pour me a glass of wine, oh what a day I've had." Gerald did as he was asked and removed the lid off the bottle of wine and then began to pour it into glasses. He then placed them on the dinner table.

Suddenly Christina produced their dinner she smiled and handed Gerald his dinner, she then said, "Here Gerald, well-roasted lamb." Gerald laughed and replied, "Well roasted lamb, my favourite." they all began laughing. After consuming their dinner or most of it, Gerald looked at the old art Nouveau clock, he then reached inside his pocket for the piece of paper with the numbers on it David had written down. Christina was busy washing dishes in the kitchen, Gerald looked to David as he turned the television on, he then said, "A couple of minutes to the euro million draw it would be rude not to check if you had won or not, the odds are pretty impressive, no one with psychic abilities has ever won, but your confidence intrigues me, nothing you do surprises me anymore."

David rushed over to the television and made sure it was the right channel. Gerald took a deep breath and said, "Right the moment is here." Gerald looked to the piece of paper; David sat next to him with great anticipation. "Look the first number it's Fifteen. Yes, you got that one right, good start, next forty-five good, next twenty-one, good that's three numbers. Next thirty-eight, yes."

Gerald became more and more excited as if he had placed the numbers on, one more number, two. Gerald jumped out of his seat, David laughed hysterically and said, "I told you I could do it."

Gerald said, "Wait, the bonus numbers, five number and eight my god you picked out all the numbers, you have powers beyond human comprehension, the jackpot." Christina entered the room and said, ", "What is all the fuss about?" Gerald then announced the news. "David, he picked out all seven numbers." Christina joined in the celebrations pouring herself another glass of wine.

All of a sudden, she stopped in her tracks and said, "Wait what are we all doing we never actually put the numbers on." All of a sudden, the words from the television echoed all around the room, there were no jackpot winners of the eighty million Jackpot, and then a knock on the door.

Christina looked at Gerald and said, "Who could that be? Hope it is not Charles and Pepe." Gerald regained his composure and then spoke in a deep voice, "Stay here whilst I answer the door." Gerald walked towards the front door, he felt a cold shiver run down his spine, fearfully he opened the front door in front of him stood two strangers dressed in black. Harry spoke in a confident voice, "Hi Sir we are a couple of Government agents, you must be Gerald, we have been knocking for a while, all we could hear was the sounds of celebrations don't tell me you have won the lottery. I never seem to win anything, anyway we are here to talk to you about your son, our superiors watched the film and we have read the report on your son's experiment, such amazing powers. Do you require us to discuss this at another time? Sounds like you were celebrating something amazing."

Gerald was not thinking straight and said, "My son has just done something truly amazing; I should not be telling you this, but he has picked out all seven numbers and it was an eighty million jackpot." Harry took a deep breath, smiled and said, "No wonder you're celebrating, I wish he was my son I could finally retire, so your now rich Mr Trump."

Gerald shrugged his shoulders and replied, "No you have got me all wrong, I never put the numbers on. Is that an American accent what is it you wanted?" Harry's facial expression changed, his face turned white as a ghost, he then said, "Oh all of a sudden I am not feeling too good, Ryan let's go, let's get out of here before I say something I shouldn't."

Harry turned pale, his face a complete expression of horror, his mind whispered get the hell out of there. Gerald looked on in disbelief as the agents turned around and proceeded to walk towards their hire car. Gerald shouts to the agents, "Wait what is the matter was it something I said?"

Harry couldn't believe what he has just witnessed, he turned to Ryan and spoke, "whilst shaking his head, "My God!" Ryan looked to Harry who is now like an erupting volcano, he then spoke once more, "Ryan did you hear what that stupid man just said?" Ryan replied, "Err something about the euro millions." Harry kicked the car and then climbed in; he punched the dashboard. Ryan got in and said, "Look calm down, hold your breath and count to ten." Harry performed the requested task counting to ten. Ryan was confused, he turned to Harry and said, "Tell me why you're angry, what happened to play it cool? You just acted like a complete fool."

Without shouting, Harry agreed and said, "You mean you never heard what that weird French guy said to me? Alright, that guy Gerald informed me his son David picked out the seven euro million numbers, they were all celebrating." Ryan laughed and said, ", "So this upset you?" Harry replied, "The jackpot was eighty million, but listen to this slowly they never put the bet on."

Ryan shook his hand and then spoke in a heightened voice, "My God! Why were they celebrating? I know I would be suicidal, what about you?" Harry replied, "Yes now you know why I was angry, eighty million, that kid's a gold mine." Ryan smiled and said, "Harry are you thinking what I am thinking? Imagine if he could predict the American lottery numbers, a cool one hundred million dollars, we could split the money down the middle fifty million dollars each."

Harry adopted a cruel smile, as they looked back at the house Gerald had returned back inside. The hire car drove off slowly, Christina turned to Gerald and said, "Who were those men?" Gerald replied, "I am not sure, they said, "they were government agents." Christina shook her head and said, "Did you ask what government?" Gerald replied, "Oh the agent talking sounded American."

David stood up, he had an uneasy feeling, he spoke in a concerned voice, "Mum, it is the dream I told you about, remember I visited the fifth dimension a creature called Cavoc warned me about men from America were going to kidnap me" Gerald looked to Christina and said, "I am very sorry, I may have put the ball in motion, I was still in a state of shock and accidentally informed the agents about the euro lottery and how David picked out all seven numbers. After that, the agent doing the talking felt sick and left."

Christina looked to Gerald, "You fool, they know David could win them riches beyond their dreams just because we would not take advantage of our son's gifts, others would." Anxiety twisted her face. Gerald laughed, putting on a brave face he said, "We are all jumping to conclusions are we not? Let's face it, David has such an unusual imagination, Cavoc and the fifth dimension! Only David could have produced such a story."

David looked at his father with an expression of horror and thought "why does he not believe me?" His Mother and Father continued with their conversation as he disappeared into the shadows and then into his bedroom. Christina looked into Gerald's eyes and said, ", "Who does he take after, imaginary friends?" Gerald pulled a face and replied, "Why me, of course, I had an imaginary friend called Sinbad." Christina shook her head and finished off her wine.

Harry and Ryan returned to their hotel, they both sat on chairs sipping their Jack Daniel's. Ryan said, "Harry come on, what do you think? You're the brains of the outfit." Harry sat resting with his hands on his knees, he then replied, "Yes you can say that again! Imagine if somehow, we could get that kid back to America with us, I reckon I could persuade him to divulge information on the winning numbers, we could collect the money then let him go. We can do it as we are Government agents."

Ryan scratched his head and then spoke, "Sounds so easy." Harry shook his head and said, "No this is not going to be easy; we need someone to do the kidnapping as his Father has seen us." Ryan had an idea, "Why don't we knock off his parents and take the lad back to America ourselves?" Harry shook his head and replied, "No we do things my way, we get someone else to do all the dirty work and then we pop up and reap the benefits."

Ryan's eyes lit up he then spoke with a confident voice, "Harry that sounds good I like that." Harry laughed and said, "I know, I will make a phone call and arrange everything." Ryan laughed and then said, "Who you going to phone?" Harry replied, "Look I will tell you later, I want you to have a little faith in me." Ryan nodded his head, "He stood up and said, "Alright Harry whatever you say."

Harry had two regular scumbags in mind, Daisy and Peter. They were scumbags, but who else could he trust? Harry stood up and then proceeded to another room, he checked his cell phone until Daisy's number came up, the two of them were a sort of item ten years earlier, she was an angel turned demon always mixing with the wrong crowd. Very soon she got mixed up in drugs and guns. Harry soon left and a dealer moved in his name was 'Pistol Whipped Peter' as he was abused as a child. His father pistol-whipped him as a teenager at the age of twenty he afflicted the same punishment on his father and put two bullets in his head for good measure.

Could a couple of homicidal maniacs pull this off? The smart money said, "yes. Harry called Daisy, a brief delay and then she answered. Harry spoke in a deep voice, "Hi this is Harry, remember me? I got a job for you and Peter what do you reckon?"

Daisy was all ears, she soon replied, "What job?" Harry smiled and said, "I want you both to kidnap a boy in Paris and take him back to the States." Daisy pulled a face and said, ", "You what?" Daisy began acting strangely, she then spoke in a strange voice, "What, I have moral responsibilities and to think you used to call me Angel?" Harry laughed and replied, "Okay how about a million each to forget your moral responsibilities?" Daisy laughed and said, "That's better, when do we get our money?" Harry then spoke with a clear, dominant voice, "Only if the kid gets to Washington D.C. in one piece, completely unharmed or the deal is off, explain this in great detail to your guy, Peter."

Daisy began to think, she then said, "Don't worry about Peter, he does as he is told, I wear the pants. Anyway, what is his true value of this kid then Agent?" Harry replied, "Mind your own business, leave for Paris immediately, do I make myself clear? I am here in Paris with Ryan remember Ryan?"

Daisy replied, "Yes who could forget that lanky streak of piss? However did he ever become your partner?" Harry laughed and then replied, "That's a good question, I wish I had an answer. Remember to phone this number when you arrive." Daisy laughed and said, "Ok job's a good one, we both got passports, we will buy some tickets and be in Paris as soon as possible, anyway thanks for thinking of me for this job." Harry laughed and replied, "To be honest with you I had no one else to ask." Daisy became angry and shouted, "You bastard! Same old Harry." She then turned off her mobile.

Harry smiled, his mind said, "now for his alibi, he always looked after number one, he walked back into the room with a broad smile. He then turned to Ryan and said, "My friend, the wheels are in motion, remember when we visited Gerald, David's father he saw me I said, "I had to leave as I was not feeling too well? I've had sickness and diarrhoea I have an alibi, you, my friend are going to the chemist to get me some tablets, remember to say to whoever serves you it is for my bedridden partner, Harry, he is in a real bad way."

Ryan shook his head and said, "Harry my God you're smart!" Harry replied, "Don't I know it, now get me some tablets, remember a nice conversation with whoever serves you from where you buy the tablets, my sick partner, Harry. Now get a move on, I want the tablets right away." With that Ryan left the room slamming the door behind him.

In Washington DC, in a slum part of the city, Daisy stood up and made herself a cup of coffee in a rundown apartment. She had long jet-black hair, her face was small and delicate, at one time she had the looks of an angel, but her lifestyle had taken its toll on her face and body.

She finished off making her coffee, a quick sip then she approached Peter who was in his thirties. He had scars on his forehead, permanent reminders of his unfortunate upbringing. He was of medium build with brown hair and matching eyes. Daisy began to laugh to herself, she then spoke in a funny voice, "Hi honey." she put her arms around him, Peter smiled and slowly opened his eyes, he had been napping, he then said, ", "Is that you, flower?" She laughed and replied, "Why no, it's me, Daisy, we got ourselves a nice job." All of a sudden Peter's eyes became fully focused, he then said, "Are you serious, no messing, what job?" Daisy replied, "Remember Harry?" Peter scanned his memory and then replied, "Oh that jerk, dirty Harry." Daisy nodded her head and said, "That's him, we need to leave for Paris immediately."

Peter shook his head and said," What you got to be kidding"? Daisy replied, "A cool one million each for kidnapping a kid, is that alright? I just thought the money would come in handy." Peter became excited and said, "Did you say one million each?" Daisy blew Peter a kiss and said, "Yes all we got to do is a little kidnapping, does it not sound good? Just think if old jerk arse is offering us a million each what's his cut twenty million?"

Peter laughed and said, "who cares? For now, once we got the kid on our patch, we can renegotiate a new deal, an extra couple of million maybe, but first things first, let's go kidnap the kid in Paris and then bring him back to the lion's den." Daisy smiled and licked her lips, she then spoke in strange voice, "Honey, remember one thing I am in charge I am the brains of the outfit we go to Paris straight away, one light bag as we are on a short stay, it's so romantic there and we, my lover boy are on our honeymoon, does that sound good?"

Peter pulled a funny face and the replied, ", ", "Sounds good to me flower." Daisy smiled and said, ", "I want you to just chill, I will get the tickets and do all the work." Peter gazed into Daisy's eyes and said, ", "My God where would I be without you?" Daisy replied, ", ", "Lost in the gutter, now get off your lazy arse and pack a few clothes, do I make myself clear?" Peter nodded and then quickly got to his feet and did as he was told.

In Paris, David lay on his bed. Suddenly Gerald opened the door, he walked over to David's bed and sat on the chair next to the old bookshelf, he then spoke in a low, calm voice, "Son, let us talk, I am sorry, but can you shed some light on the dream you had who or what is Cavoc?"

David sat up in his bed remembering the dream as if it was a couple of hours of ago, he then replied, "Cavoc is a sort of creature that lives in the fifth dimension, there is a balance of good and evil throughout history he has walked amongst men, he said, " I was of the bloodline that is why I have such amazing powers, he mentioned David Burns, he lived in Paris also, but he died in England after he was betrayed by a demonic figure called Mabus. He mentioned Nostradamus, the book of predictions he wrote in fifteen fifty-five that was a reward from Cavoc, he made those predictions and Nostradamus took the credit. He also told me when the world will end."

Gerald sat in a trance-like state, imagine if David was telling the truth. Gerald then asked, "When will the world end what year?" David replied, "Oh he said, "the world would end in twenty-twenty five." Gerald believed in his son's powers and said, "I know, I will research this character, David Burns, if he exists, I would be inclined to believe you, he mentioned the American agents kidnapping you when will this happen?"

David replied, "I am not sure, but I was told there was nothing I or anyone else could do to prevent this." Gerald scratched his head then spoke in a heightened voice, "We shall see, I want you to go to sleep, tomorrow

I shall have some answers." David smiled and said, "Thank you, Father, for at least listening to my story, oh one more thing Cavoc said, "Saint Francis would protect me." Gerald laughed and said, "Alright son."

He then left the room and walked downstairs; he started his research on the computer. Christina crept up behind Gerald and began to massage his shoulders, Gerald whispered, "Oh that's better, you have such healing hands, you should do this for a living." Christina smiled, then proceeded to give Gerald a head massage, she then enquired what her husband was doing.

Gerald replied, "Oh I promised to research a certain David burns who once lived in Paris." Christina Shook her head and then spoke in a confused voice, ", "Should you be encouraging him, Sinbad?" Gerald laughed and then replied, "Maybe I should not have told you, I also had an imaginary friend we once flew about Paris on his magic carpet, anyway enough of me, this is David we are talking about and I do not see it like that, maybe he is telling the truth. He mentioned those two American agents."

Christina then said, "Sorry that I find it all hard to believe." She then left her husband alone and ventured up to bed.

Back in the Hotel Ryan returned with the medicine, he handed it to Harry, he then said, ", "Look, before you say anything, your instructions were carried out to the letter, the guy who served me spoke English." He then sat down talking to Harry, he then asked a question.

"Harry you never told me who is doing the kidnapping." Harry replied, "I know, I believe it is now time to tell you, remember Daisy the girl I once dated?" Ryan remembered her oh so well, he then replied, "You mean Daisy the regular pistol-packing flower? I reckon you have also invited 'Pistol Whipped Peter'."

Harry nodded his head. Ryan could not believe his ears, and then carried on speaking in a raised voice, ", "My God! You must have been desperate." Harry laughed and said, ", "Yes, there was no one else daft enough to take on the job. Listen to what I am about to say, they will arrive in Paris tomorrow, if everything goes to plan soon you will meet them. Here I have written down a plan, I want you to give it to them it has the kid's address."

Ryan smiled and said, "What about weapons?" Harry laughed and then replied, "They do not need weapons, both Peter and Daisy are weapons, either one of them could overpower that man I spoke to at the front door, I don't want no one getting hurt, they will be tied up until they are out of the country. We shall be staying a little longer as we cannot be implicated in the kidnapping, after all, I am still bedridden. It must have been some kind of virus."

Ryan rubbed his eyes then said, ", "Why don't you take some medicine then?" Harry replied, ", ", "Because there is nothing wrong with me you clown." Ryan laughed and said, ", "I know, I was only joking, but how will they get the kid back to the States?"

Harry reached for a brown envelope and then said, ", "I want you to give them this." Ryan took the envelope from Harry's hand and said, ", "What is in it, Harry?" Harry smiled and replied, ", ", "The plan and money, the kid I reckon will have a passport if not, I have placed an address where one can be forged. As soon as they have kidnapped the kid, I want them out of Paris as soon as possible. Open it tomorrow."

Harry then produced another bottle of Jack Daniel's, he then poured it into two glasses and said, ", "Okay it's nightcap time." Ryan took a drink, Harry took a sip of his drink then looked to Ryan and said, ", "You have been with Cindy for ten years, that my friend is some record for our line of work." Ryan shook his head and replied, "My time flies! Guess I haven't got the curse yet." Harry scratched his head and then replied, "Yes I know, two failed marriages, kids I don't bother to see, I know all about bad luck, it follows me around, it's something I just can't shake off. My problem is I am so hard to live with, always thinking of number one." Ryan pulled a face and said, "Nothing's changed on that score, remember your first wife? Didn't she leave you at Christmas, taking the kids with her?"

Harry took another sip and then replied, "Yeh she said, " I was a scrooge and a mean bastard because I didn't buy the kids any presents, to be honest with you, my mind was on the job, maybe I was lost in a case." Ryan took a sip of his drink and then said, "Was it a suitcase?" Harry choked on his drink as they both burst out into laughter. Ryan then said, ", "Your second wife, didn't she catch you sleeping with her best friend?" Harry replied, "Yeah it was just a misunderstanding."

Ryan was confused and said, "How do you mean?" Harry replied, "She wasn't meant to be there, she told me she was going on a business trip to Florida and she would be away for five days." Ryan laughed and said, "Guess she came back early." Harry finished off his drink then said, Yeah I got caught red-handed in the act."

Ryan finished off his drink, then poured out another two drinks and then said, "I bet she was pissed, I remember she was a big lady." Harry shook his head and replied, "Yeah, I had to arrest her, the bitch attacked me with a carving knife, I restrained her and then called for lots of back up."

Ryan gazed into Harry's eyes and said, "Whatever happened to her?" Harry took a deep breath and replied, "Oh she went completely bonkers and ended up in a nut farm, do you know what? I blame all of this on my lousy childhood, I was beaten and abused at the hands of my drunken father."

Ryan scratched his nose and then said, "Whatever happened to your family." "Oh, my Mother died God rest her soul, after that my father became worse and shot himself in the head." Ryan shook his head and said, "Such a tragic ending." Harry disagreed and said, "For who?" I ended up living with my aunty Sue, she spoilt me rotten. I remember the seventies growing up in the seventies we had a black and white television, I recall my Father, he was in love with Sergeant Bilko."

Ryan laughed and said, "My God Harry! You never said, "your father was gay." Harry shook his head and then replied, "He wasn't you schmuck, it was a comedy programme, in fact, it was a very funny tv comedy, I remember listening to his howls of laughter. It was the only time I heard him laugh."

Ryan took a sip of his drink and said, "Sorry Harry I have never heard of Sergeant Bilko." Harry took a sip of his drink, he then looked to Ryan and said, "Okay smart ass, do you remember a series called Happy Days with a cool guy in it called the Fonz, played by Henry Winkler?" Ryan replied, "No" Harry then said, "Cunningham you nerd." Ryan shrugged his shoulders and said, "Not really."

Harry scanned his memory and then said, "How about the Waltons? Everyone in America has heard of the Waltons." Ryan pulled a face and replied, "I haven't." Harry shook his head and said, "Goodnight John-boy, my God you're such hard work, are there any old tv shows that spring to your mind?" Ryan replied, "Mash" Harry shook his head and said, ", "No we're not talking about food, we're talking about tv shows."

Ryan put on a serious face and said to Harry, "Are you having me on?" Harry laughed and replied, "Yes, I remember Mash, good old hot lips Houlihan." Ryan took a deep breath and said, "Yeah, do you know what used to make me laugh as a kid?" Harry replied, "I don't know but I have a feeling you're going to tell me." Ryan smiled and said, "Laurel and Hardy." Harry took a sip of his drink and said, "Yeah now you're talking, classic comedy."

Ryan picked up the bottle and filled up their glasses, he then took a sip, Harry then said, ", "I bet you can't remember the first single you ever brought." Ryan replied, "No I cannot." Harry laughed and said, "I can as if it was yesterday, it was REO Speedwagon, 'keep on loving you', do you know what year it was?" Ryan laughed and replied, "Was it in Jurassic times?" Harry shook his head and replied, "Smartass, I am only fifty you know, I was born in the sixties that was the great time when I arrived on this glorious planet." Ryan laughed and said, "Harry does that mean you're drunk?"

Harry laughed and then replied, "No but I am getting there." He then took another sip of his drink. Ryan turned to Harry and said, "Remember that time we had a pop quiz in our early days it was our first assignment in Amsterdam?" Harry laughed and replied, "Yeah, Cocaine Charlie the chimp boy, did we bust his ass, can you remember how many kilos he was shipping to the states?"

Ryan replied, "Heck no, it was a long time ago." Harry rubbed his left eye and said, "I can't remember either, the main thing was we got the scumbag, from that day on we just kept busting ass." Ryan laughed and said, "Those were the days my friend." With that, Harry suddenly broke out into song, "I hoped they would never end, we would sing and dance forever and a day, those where the days my friend."

Ryan suddenly burst out into laughter he then said, "My God Harry! Your singing is terrible." Harry shook his head in disagreement, he then said, "I am the king of the karaoke." Ryan took a sip of his drink then replied, "Bullshit! You can't sing and you know nothing about music." Harry took a sip of his drink then replied, "Okay smartass, let us have a quick quiz on that subject, music, I will name a singer or group and you will name their best hit." Ryan laughed and then said, "Okay Harry shall we proceed?"

Harry said, "Michael Jackson." Ryan replied, "Wanna be starting something." Harry shook his head in confusion and then replied, "What do you mean wanna be starting something?" Ryan shook his and replied, "That's the name of the song, my favourite hit by Michael Jackson." Harry laughed and then said, "Elvis Presley." Ryan replied, "in seconds, "Hound dog." Harry scratched his head then replied, "Who you calling a Hound dog?" Ryan shook his head and replied, "No it's the name of the song I like." Harry laughed and then said, "I know I was only kidding okay, REO Speedwagon." Ryan shook his head then spoke in a confused voice, "Harry who are they? I reckon they are a bit before my time." Harry took a deep breath and replied, "I gave you the answer five minutes ago remember the first single I ever brought? However, did you get a job working for the CIA?"

Ryan laughed and replied, "Harry I was only joking, 'I am going to keep on loving you'." Harry laughed and replied, "Get lost you faggot." "Okay Ryan, Tina turner describe me?" Ryan replied, "'simply the best'." Harry laughed and then said, "Yeah now you're learning. Did I ever tell you I once met her? I've met lots of celebrities over the years, remember that guy out of Malt Loaf?" Ryan laughed and then replied, "You mean Meat Loaf." Harry smiled and said, "That's the one, a couple of rookie traffic cops pulled him over for speeding on his Harley Davidson motorcycle, they informed me he was riding like a bat out of hell."

Ryan spoke in a raised voice, "Shut up Harry, I don't believe a word you're saying." Harry smiled and then carried on with his story. "Anyway, I got him off with the speeding fine and he gave me a signed picture of himself, I then sold it on eBay and made seventy dollars, happy days. Oh, anyway back to our quiz, The Monkees."

Ryan replied, "Daydream Believer." Harry replied, "I sure am" he then said, "Simon and Garfunkel?" Ryan replied, "Mrs Robinson, Jesus loves you more than you could know." Harry yawned and then said, "I know he does, he then blinked, his mind became paralysed by the side effects of the Jack Daniel's, he stood up and then fell onto his bed. He was soon in a state of unconsciousness.

Ryan got to his feet he slurred his speech, "Goodnight Harry." He then did the same, falling onto his bed, the Jack Daniel's had, had the desired effect. They were soon both fast asleep.

The following morning soon came around and they both lay fast asleep. Daisy and Peter arrived in Paris they pronounced their love for each other whilst strolling through the Airport terminal. They were both dressed in casual clothes, Peter carried a small bag, travel light that was the order of the day. Very soon they had left the Airport, Daisy turned to Peter and said, "Did you know this is one of the most romantic cities?" Peter turned and gave her a romantic kiss and then suddenly the sun appeared in all of its radiant glory, Peter shaded his eyes and then said, "I need my sexy shades."

Peter reached into his bag then produced a pair of designer shades, he quickly put them on as he knew Daisy loved him wearing them, she gazed for a minute then said, "My God you sure look sexy in shades." Peter got all excited and flicked his hair, he then replied, ", "you reckon?" Daisy blew him a kiss and replied, "Come closer you sexy beast." Daisy pulled him closer and then kissed him passionately on the lips, she then pushed him away and said, "Okay pleasure time is now over, it's time for business, time to call dirty Harry."

She then reached inside her pocket and then produced her mobile phone; she then rang Harry. They both lay asleep suffering from the side effects of drinking too much Jack Daniel's. Harry's mobile rang out over and over again, he lay shaken and dazed and then panic fears fluttered his mind the noise began pounding in his ears, his anger then erupted like a volcano he then began screaming like a madman, "Where the fuck is my mobile phone?" Ryan jumped out of his skin and then cried out, "God damn you, Harry, it's over there where you left it."

Harry got out of bed and then picked up his mobile he answered the call, "Shit is that you Daisy? My God you got here quick." Daisy laughed and replied, "You took your time answering my call, oh what's that smell on your breath, I reckon you have been on the whisky am I right?"

Harry replied, "Ok smart arse, you know me, and I know you." Daisy then said, "Harry back to the real world, me and Peter have arrived in this fair city is that clear?" Harry replied, "No I have to disagree, it's gloomy and it stinks." Daisy burst out into laughter, she then said, "Harry you're showing your age again, a grumpy old man."

Harry became angry and replied, "Shit why does everyone keep saying I am over the hill?" Daisy smiled and replied, "Sorry the truth must hurt." Harry interrupted and said, "Look, shut up about my age, we all grow old let's get back to business." Daisy agreed and then said, "How is your dumb sidekick? Has he also been on Jack's juice? Where is the plan? He should have been here awaiting our arrival do you agree?"

Harry replied, "Look you arrived early, that's something I wasn't expecting, look take in the sights I will send Ryan over to pick you up as soon as possible, he will give you the plan and drop you off at a small bed and breakfast establishment near to where you are to do the job. Is all of this understood?" Daisy replied, "What is the magic word? Something we need, it wasn't cheap getting here do you know what I mean?" Harry replied, "Oh, it slipped my mind with the plan, is cash enough to get you out of here okay?"

Daisy replied, "My, the same old Harry always a perfectionist." Harry forced a smile and replied, "Look, Daisy, I demand perfection." Daisy then hung up. Harry then turned his attention to Ryan and said, "Shit look at you, a cold shower and a gallon of coffee will put you straight, come on get a move on they're waiting for you." Harry sat back as Ryan stood up feeling the worst for wear, he gazed at Harry and said, "My God Harry, I still feel intoxicated." Harry replied, "Yes I know that is why you need a cold shower whilst I fix you a coffee." Ryan agreed and then moved gingerly towards the shower.

Harry listened as the shower became operational, he then laughed to himself as Ryan cried out as the cold water began to patter against his body. Harry made three cups of coffee; he began to drink one the other two were for Ryan. A few minutes later he returned from his ordeal fully dressed and ready for action, but first, he needed coffee.

Harry laughed and said, "My that was quick your cups of coffee are there." Ryan replied, "Okay Harry you're right we must not keep them waiting, the cold shower did the trick I now feel wide awake."

Ryan then began to drink the coffee, Harry finished off his coffee then spoke in a dominant voice, "Okay I want you to drink both cups of coffee and be on your way to the airport, you will be a little late as my mother used to say better late than never." Ryan smiled and said, "My, Harry your mum was sure smart." Harry shook his head and replied, "No I have to disagree, she married my father remember?" Ryan replied, "Oh yeah, I never thought of that."

Harry stood up and smiled he then said, "Okay Ryan, Paris is famous for what magnificent structure on display?" Ryan replied, "Oh that's easy it's the Trifle tower." Harry laughed out loud and said, "I reckon you are thinking of food; I believe the name of the tower is Eiffel, not Trifle." Ryan shrugged his shoulders and replied, "It must have been that ice-cold shower." Harry scratched his head and replied, "Tower, shower and now it is the hour be on your way as it is time for play." Ryan laughed and left for the airport with the brown envelope.

Peter became more and more impatient anxiety twisted his face he gazed into Daisy's eyes and said, "Where the hell is Ryan?" Daisy tried her best to muster a confident smile, she then replied, "Must be running a little late, won't you to calm down honey? Very soon we will be very rich, and I have decided what I am going to do with the money."

Peter was now calm and all ears he replied, "What sugar?" Daisy smiled and replied, "I fancy an island in the Caribbean." Peter became excited, he then said, "You must have read my mind because I fancy the same what shall we call it?" Daisy replied, "Why, Daisy and Peter of course." Peter shook his head and said, "Why not Peter and Daisy's island?" Daisy rolled her eyes and replied, "Well honey bun, Daisy and Peter's island has a sort of ring to it."

Peter scratched his head for a few seconds and then agreed with Daisy. She then took a deep breath whilst gazing all around she then turned to Peter and said, "Look over there at that little old lady carrying a freshly baked baguette, or over there at that boy walking proud showing off his new Lacoste polo shirt. Did you know all of these people worship the Eiffel tower?" Peter stood confused, he then replied, "Are you sure?" Daisy replied, "Well I have you know, I once read this fact in a magazine." Peter moved forward and kissed Daisy on the cheek and said, "My, you're so smart, where would I be without you?" Daisy replied, "That's an easy one, you would be pure and simple gutter trash, and don't you ever forget it."

Peter humbled himself before her, he then said, "My God! I love you, give me a kiss, Daisy." She put her arms around him and said, "Let us radiate an atmosphere of love, after all, we are in Paris."

She then flung herself upon him kissing him passionately on the lips. The romance was caught short as the noise of a car horn began to echo in their ears, Daisy let go of Peter and turned around, she then spoke in a loud voice, "My God! It's Ryan, no peace for the wicked. Remember we must stay cool, just think of the money." Peter agreed and they both made their way to the parked black Citroen automobile.

Daisy got into the front seat as Peter got into the back, Daisy then put on her best false smile and then said, "Hi Ryan longtime no see what's up with the old man?" Ryan laughed and replied, "He ain't feeling too well, sickness and diarrhoea." Daisy laughed and then said, "Oh my, that sounds like a virus of sorts, is he suffering from a huge hangover the Jack Daniel's variety?" Ryan nodded as he then started up the car and began to drive towards their destination.

Daisy continued talking, "That old guy will never change, so sad, anyway back to business." Ryan agreed and then handed Daisy the plan, she took hold of the envelope, she then opened it up and said, "Unbelievable! Harry must have a virus he's gone and filled it full of cash." Daisy loved the feel of fresh notes as we all do, she pulled a funny face then said, "Okay Ryan baby where are you taking us?" Ryan replied, "Well I am taking you to a nice bed and breakfast where you can check-in under false names, Harry will want you to read his plan again and again and then you carry out the kidnapping. When you have achieved your goal just contact Harry is that all clear?"

Daisy replied, "Crystal clear big boy." Ryan shook his head, his mind whispered: "what have I let myself into?" Suddenly they arrived at their destination, Ryan pulled over, he then turned to Daisy and said, "Okay this is the place." Peter got out first, he was acting on strict orders, just stay cool.

Daisy blew Ryan a kiss as she got out of the car she then said, "Okay until later bye bye lover boy." Ryan was wearing designer shades, he blinked shook his head then pulled off in a hurry. Peter approached Daisy and said, "Why I am all confused I thought I was your lover boy?" Daisy replied, "You are honey, it was all but a joke, but now no messing about we need to put on our serious heads on and read these darn plans."

Peter put on a sad face and said, "My, Daisy you know I can't read." Daisy shrugged her shoulders and replied, "Oh well nobody's perfect, I will have to read for the two of us." Daisy and Peter then checked in and then made their way to the room. Daisy opened the door and they both entered, Peter sat down as Daisy closed the door and then pulled out the plan from within the brown envelope. She began reading, suddenly panic fears started to flutter through her mind, her anger rose and then she spoke in a raised voice, "Moral responsibilities, no extreme violence that is what gets the job done quicker, everybody knows that."

Peter shook his head and replied, "I didn't." Daisy gazed into his eyes and said, "Well honey you are the exception to the rule." Peter was confused and replied, "What does that mean?" Daisy replied, "It means you are special with a certain need for enlightenment on a regular basis." Peter was now even more confused, he scratched his head and replied, "My, Daisy where did you say you were educated?" Daisy replied, "No honey, I am self-taught, anyway Peter I've been using extreme violence all my life and look where it has gotten me."

Peter smiled and replied, "You're right babe you got me, babe." Daisy shook her head in disbelief then said, "My God, Peter you say the most stupid things." Peter bowed his head like a naughty schoolboy he then said, "My, Daisy does this mean you and me are no longer an item?" Daisy replied, "Of course me and you are still an item, you just need to think more before you speak."

Peter said, "he was sorry, he then said, "thinking ain't one of my strong points." Daisy agreed and then said, "I blame your Father, it's all his fault." Peter was once more confused, he replied, "Why is it my father's fault?" Daisy replied, "Don't you remember being pistol-whipped as a small boy?" Peter replied, "Oh yeah I still get headaches, but I sorted him out in the end, bullets to the head and then lay dead."

Daisy pulled a face and then said, "Don't you fret honey, he got what he deserved." Peter smiled and said, "You're right Daisy, what goes around comes around." Daisy then scratched her head for a few seconds, she then gazed into Peter's eyes and said, "Yeah that makes sense must be one of those rare occasions when you say something that adds up." Peter laughed and replied, "Why thank you Daisy math's wasn't one of my strong subjects at school, what is next in the plan?"

Daisy replied, "We got the address and a map to get there it's not far from here, the three of them live there, Gerald the father, Christina the mother and their son

David who is fifteen years of age. His parents are posh, and we do not need weapons to overpower them, they ain't streetwise like us we are hard as nails."

Peter nodded in agreement then said, "You're right Daisy, I bet they never got pistol-whipped whey they were kids." Daisy replied, "I know honey, I reckon you are quite unique one of a kind, we must remember to get the kid's passport, we will be out of this country before any alarm has been raised." Peter took a deep breath and then smiled, he then spoke, "What happens if the kid doesn't cooperate?" Daisy replied, "That's easy honey, we kill his parents one by one is that okay?"

Peter replied, "My, Daisy you are so smart, I reckon you were put on God's earth to look out for me, my destiny." Daisy laughed and said, ", "I wouldn't go that far." Peter smiled and replied, "Well Daisy how far would you go?" Daisy yawned and then replied, "Oh I am tired, let's move on from this sad conversation, let's just concentrate on the plan at hand."

Peter shook his head and then spoke in an angry voice, "I reckon we go do this thing now what do you reckon?" Daisy replied, "No, Harry wants us to get some shut-eye first. Peter became angry and impatient, he then spoke with a raised voice, "Fuck Harry, I say we do this now, his plan ain't worth shit from now on I am doing things my way just like that singer, Frank Sinatra." Daisy was shocked at his outburst she remained calm and said, "You must be joking, more like Nancy, okay big boy let's do it, one minute you're nice then angry, you remind me of that strange British guy." Peter was confused and asked, "Which one?" Daisy replied, "Jekyll and Hyde." Peter again asked, "Which one?" Daisy put her hands over her face she then dropped her arms and replied, "Look you are starting to piss me off, don't say another word, from now on I do all the talking, you just listen understood? please just nod."

Peter did as he was told and nodded his head. Daisy then left as Peter picked up the small bag, he then followed her out of the bed and breakfast, she looked at the map and then pointed to the direction of David's house. Daisy turned to Peter and said, ", "Right just listen this is the plan, let me do all the talking, I will put on a posh accent as we are working for a magazine in the States, as soon as he gets wise to us you jump him understood?"

Peter nodded and replied, "Yes Daisy." The weather was cloudy and overcast a cool breeze blew litter along the pavement, Peter became inpatient once more, he turned to Daisy and said, "You sure we ain't lost?" Daisy shook her head and replied, "Look Peter stop being stupid, it's a mile up that road is that okay?" Peter replied, "Oh good, I need a drink do you need one?" Daisy replied, "Look we are keeping a low profile, you drink when I drink do you understand?" Peter replied, "Okay whatever you say, is it okay if we hold hands?" Daisy agreed and Peter took hold of her hand as they walked towards their destination. Daisy smiled and then looked into Peter's eyes and said, "My, don't you think this place is romantic?" Peter replied, "You're right, but

I reckon romance is such thirsty work." Daisy let go of his hand and then spoke in an angry voice, "Shut it, you're beginning to get on my nerves."

Very soon they arrived at the house, Daisy took a deep breath then walked up to the front door, she knocked then turned to Peter with a sly wink, a brief delay and then Gerald opened the door.

Daisy revealed her most sickly smile and then spoke, "Hi sir my name's Rebecca and with me my photographer Simon, we're here to do an interview with your son David, we're from the New York Times." Gerald looked at them both in total disbelief and replied, "How can you take photographs you have no camera?" Before Gerald could react, Daisy punched him in the face, Gerald cried out in pain, blood pouring from a broken nose.

Daisy grew up in a rough neighbourhood and knew how to fight, Peter then threw a right hook to the side of Gerald's head, he fell to the ground, dazed and bewildered. Peter then jumped on Gerald adopting a headlock, he then said, "Any trouble from you and the kid gets it." Gerald started to struggle violently throwing Peter to the ground, as he got to his feet Daisy picked up a large vase and then smashed it over Gerald's head. He fell to the floor like a tonne of bricks, knocked clean out. Peter then jumped to his feet all of a sudden Christina walked into the room, she was listening to a personal stereo and hadn't heard the commotion until the vase broke.

Christina looked at her husband laying motionless, blood pouring from a head wound panic fears fluttered her mind, she then said, "My God! What have you done to my husband?" Daisy replied, "Look, lady, stay cool or you will get the same, understood?"

Christina was a cool lady, she then replied, "Look is this a robbery?" Daisy replied, "Yes just want the money and your cooperation, start off by helping your husband, he had a nasty fall."

Christina's mind whispered," what about David?" He was in his bedroom reading his books. Christina looked at her husband and then said, "He needs an ambulance will you call one?" Daisy shook her head, then replied in an angry voice, "Are you for real? This a robbery!"

Christina sat down next to her husband, then examined the wound, she and wiped away the blood, she then stood up and said, "Can I at least clean the wound and put a bandage around his head?"

Daisy could not believe her ears; this was robbery for God's sake! Christina gazed into her cold eyes, her mind whispered, "Oh such strange homicidal behaviour." Christina stood motionless with an expression of horror, suddenly a cruel smile followed by anger that erupted like a volcano. Daisy shouted, "I want a rope to tie you up now!" Her piercing voice, "echoed all over the house, she then turned to Peter and said, "Go with her and get some rope."

David lay on his bed, he heard the shouting and fearfully walked down the stairs with an uneasy feeling, he opened the door and looked on with a shade of terror, was this what Cavoc had warned him about? Who was this mysterious stranger with a cruel smile and wild eyes? Daisy turned and saw David standing next to the door, she then spoke in a soft calming voice, "Hi David, I need you to come over here."

David remembered Cavoc's words, "You cannot change destiny." He knew there was nothing he could do to change destiny. He put on a brave face and replied, "Alright I am coming, do not harm my parents." Daisy laughed and then said, "Good you and me we're going to get on fine, a cooperative kid, now there's a novelty."

David stood beside her, then looked to the corner of the room, laying on the floor was his father, and then Peter appeared with Christina, she looked at David and said, "My son, are you alright? She hasn't hurt you, has she?" David replied, "No mum, just stay calm and cooperate with them."

Peter looked to David and said, "God, I wish you were my son, you're so smart." And then Daisy raised her ugly head and then spoke with a voice, "of malice, "Look, less of the chit chat we got a job to do, you, Christina sit down on the chair."

Christina sat down whilst Peter produced the rope, he then tied her up to the chair. Christina looked to her husband laying on the floor, she then spoke in a concerned voice, "What about Gerald?" Daisy replied, "Look, lady, once we are out of here, we will call an ambulance."

"One more thing, I am telling you, David is not going anywhere, you said it was a robbery, not a kidnapping."

Daisy with pure evil in her eyes replied, "Look, lady, I am not known for my patience, I can be a nasty bitch when I want to be." Christina looked into her cold eyes and said, "Yes, I bet you can, you look like you are enjoying yourself." Daisy laughed out loud and then said, "You have such a pretty face, I know, why don't I get me a knife from the kitchen."

David looked to his mother trying hard to stay calm, he then spoke out, "Look, destiny cannot be changed, I must go with them, I know where the passport is." Peter smiled and said, "What a smart kid." David walked over to the cabinet and announced it was in the top drawer, Daisy opened the top drawer, inside three passports, she looked at them all. Daisy then said, "Bingo! I got David's passport."

David looked up to Daisy and said, "I promise to cooperate if you telephone for an ambulance on the way to the airport, will you do that?" Daisy replied, "How did you know we were going to the airport?" Peter shook his head and said, "My God! That's one smart kid."

Daisy laughed out loud and then turned to Peter and said, "Peter oh, I mean simple Simon, don't be dumb the passport it's obvious where we are going." Peter replied, "Oh yeah, okay kid I got my mobile, I will call for an ambulance when we get there, let's go."

Daisy grabbed hold of David pulling him to the front door they then left. Christina tried to escape her bonds, but Peter had tied them several times, there was no escape.

They all went outside, Peter closed the door behind him, Daisy then looked to David and said, ", "Right kid, I am your auntie, if anyone asks, we are your auntie and uncle understood?" David nodded his head in agreement. Peter started to walk ahead and hailed down a taxi, it pulled over as Daisy grabbed hold of David's hand and they all got in the taxi, the driver asked where you would like to go?" Daisy smiled and said, "The airport, get us there as quick as possible and I will give you extra money."

The driver replied, "Okay madam." He then put his foot down, driving faster and faster towards the airport. He was of medium build with a strange black moustache and heavy dark eyebrows. David looked into Daisy's eyes and said, "What about my Father? Remember the phone call?" Daisy replied, "Patience kid, patience." The taxi weaved in and out of the traffic, Daisy looked to Peter and said, "Our mission was a complete success, we will soon have the kid on our turf."

Back at the house, Christina continued to try and free herself without success. All of a sudden, the telephone rang, Christina remembered she was supposed to meet her sister for a drink at a bar five miles from their house. Uncharacteristically the cool lady felt a red mist descending, anxiety began to twist her face, perspiration was leaking from all over her body, with wild strength she continued to try and escape her bonds. The phone continued to ring and then it stopped, her mind whispered maybe her sister Marion may call around. She then looked at Gerald, he was still out cold, he had blood around his nose and head.

The taxi pulled up at the airport, David then looked at Peter and said, "What about the phone call?" Peter replied, "Just wait, kid." David looked into his livid eyes; Peter had a square forehead across it he bared the scars of his childhood.

Daisy paid the taxi driver and then jumped out of the cab, she laughed and said, "Soon be home, Peter." David looked to Daisy and said, "I thought his name was Simon." Daisy glanced at David then with a heightened voice, she replied, "Do not get smart kid." Daisy then got them all return tickets they all walked through the airport terminal, and then to the check-in. The check-in assistant looked them up and down and said, "No cases to check in?" Daisy replied, "No it was a very brief stay, just got this small bag." The check-in assistant then said, "Can I see your passports?"

The woman was tall, complete with raven coloured hair and green eyes, she gazed towards David and said, "You look really anxious is this your first flight?" Before David could answer, Daisy, replied, "You're right it is his first flight, I am afraid he's a little shy, don't say much do you son?" David nodded in agreement. She then said, "How are all of you related?" Daisy put on a false smile and replied to the question, "That's a good question, I am his aunty I am taking him to see the

White House. He's staying for a week's vacation and then returning is that alright with you?"

The check-in assistant handed back the passports and tickets, she then replied, "Alright, wait in the departure lounge until your flight comes up." Daisy smiled and said, "Thank you, have a nice day."

David was now tired, he looked up to Daisy for the last time and said, "Remember the ambulance?" Daisy replied, "Look, kid, I lied so don't you mention it again." David shook his head knowing his words were falling on deaf and daft ears.

Back at the Hotel Ryan sat talking to Harry, both drinking ice-cold beers. Ryan laughed as he finished off his beer he then said, "My, that's cool it hits the spot. Hey, Harry, yeah about those couple of morons you hired for the job to be honest with you I can't say I trust them." Harry replied, "Look, Ryan, I was desperate, either we got them to do it or we did it ourselves. I just don't think we could have pulled it off being CIA agents."

All of a sudden, Harry received a phone call, the phone rang out and Harry answered it straight away. "Hi, is that you Daisy? What's up?" Daisy replied, "It's done, the job is done." Harry replied, in disbelief, "What? you didn't waste no time." Daisy laughed and the replied, "We are all just boarding the aircraft now soon be back in the States complete with the kid." Harry then said, ", "My God! You did it, no one hurt?" Daisy replied, "No, the father fell and banged his head, that's about it. The mother is tied up, we should be home before the alarm is raised."

Harry smiled and said, "Good, you done good, okay make sure nothing happens to the kid, I'll phone you when our work is done here bye." Harry hung up and then broke the good news to Ryan "They got the kid and are now about to board for a flight home to Washington DC." Ryan was as shocked as Harry, he blinked and then said, "Maybe I was wrong they moved so fast."

Harry went to place the mobile into his pocket when it started to ring again, Harry answered it straight away. "Oh, Hi Chief Mellor." Ryan's face became contorted and distraught, "What is happening, why haven't you called me? What progress have you made?" Harry replied, "To be completely honest Sir, none, I have been bedridden with a virus for the last couple of days."

The Chief's anger rose and rose, he then said, "Are you taking the piss out of me?" Harry replied, "No Sir, not at all." The Chief then said, "How you are feeling now, drinking beer in a bar?" Harry replied, "No Sir, we ain't in no bar I just got out of bed." The Chief then said, "what's Ryan been doing?" Harry replied, "What he does best, just remember we are a team we cover each other's backs; he's been my wet nurse back and forward getting me medicine to aid my recovery, I must admit I am now on the mend."

Chief Mellor sat listening in disbelief, it was now his turn to have his say, "Well Harry, I suggest you do your job or when you return to the States you won't have one, and you can kiss your pension goodbye do you understand?" Harry replied, "Loud and clear Chief Mellor, talking to you has reminded me about the harsh reality of life, I will do what you say straight away."

Harry then hung up, Ryan shook his head and then spoke in a low voice, "My God! Mellor sounds pissed really, how bad is it?" Harry replied, "We got another alibi, the Chief believed us, he said, "We got to get over to David's house immediately if not sooner is that ok?" Ryan replied, "But Harry, David's not there." Harry laughed and then said, ", "I know he ain't there Dumbo, we had him kidnapped, but no one else knows, we got a game to play and we must both play by the rules, in other words, let me do all the talking, understood?" Ryan nodded and said, ", "yes."

Harry drank some more beer and then said, "Let's get a few hours shut-eye." Ryan agreed and they both got into their beds and fell asleep.

Back at the house, Christina was fast asleep, many hours had passed by and then sunset, she suddenly opened her eyes, she then heard a knock on the door, it was her sister Marion. Christina started to shout, "Help," as she shouted, Gerald moaned placing his left hand on his head, Gerald slowly got to his feet and walked over to the door in a state of confusion, he opened the door it was Marian, she put her arms around Gerald and said, "What has happened? Gerald, what has happened? Where are Christina and David?" Gerald replied, "Inside, Christina is tied up."

Marion remained cool and said, "Alright I shall call the emergency services whilst you untie Christina." Marion produced her mobile phone and then called for help whilst Gerald helped his wife. Marion spoke, calm and clear, "Come immediately, there has been a break-in." She gave the address and then hung up, she then rushed over to her sister as Gerald freed his wife from the chair he then said, "Where is David?" Christina replied, "He has been kidnapped by two Americans, a man and woman."

Gerald then said, "What is it money they were after?" Christina replied, "They did not say." Gerald then felt dizzy and sat down nursing a headache. The bleeding had stopped. Christina thanked her sister and then rushed over to her husband, and then suddenly the sound of the emergency services echoed all around their dwelling. The police and paramedics raced to the property, the paramedics helped Gerald, one of them said, "We need to take you to the hospital you will need stitches and an x-ray."

Suddenly, a tall figure appeared light brown hair moustache a weather-beaten face and a matching brown jacket. He scanned all around, he then said, "Hurry out of the house, I want no contamination of the crime scene." A clear voice of authority. Christina and Marion moved towards the front followed by Gerald, and then a dominant voice, "My name is Inspector Francis, I shall be heading up this investigation, your name is?" Christina replied, "My name is Christina, and this is my sister, Marion. Two Americans, a man and a woman have kidnapped my son, David, you must save him."

The Inspector replied, "Americans you said Americans? Please excuse me for a minute, I will alert all the airports." Francis reached inside his pocket and produced a mobile phone, he then alerted the head office about the kidnapping situation, he then turned to and said, "Christina, your husband is going to hospital, one you can go with him or you can help me find these two Americans that have caused your family such grief, are you alright to accompany me to the station and give me a statement and a description of these Americans or do you need medical attention?"

Christina looked to the sister and then to the inspector, she then replied, "Of course, the sooner you have a description of them the more chance you will have of finding them is that correct?"

The inspector replied, "Madam, that is correct." Christina looked to her sister, she embraced her and thanked her for her help.

Inspector Francis looked to Christina and said, "Time is of the essence with a kidnapping, the forensic team will be here shortly, they will find any clues to the identity of these two Americans."

Christina took his advice and rushed off, waving to her sister as the inspector guided her to his car. They both got in, he then put on his siren and drove hastily towards the station, he put his foot down on the gas pedal, weaving in and out of the traffic, passing lots of police officers searching for David. The inspector was dedicated to his job he believed in true justice.

They soon arrived at the police station; the inspector parked his car then rushed Christina towards the interview room. They walked through the busy police station. The inspector suddenly came to a halt, he turned to Christina and said, ", "Okay, we will conduct the interview in room five."

He opened the door as Christina followed the inspector, he showed her to a seat, he then asked her if she required a drink. Christina replied, "Yes a glass of water." The Inspector left the room for a brief second and then returned with a glass of water.

The door opened once more as Sergeant Canter entered, he had bulged shoulders and was of medium height, light brown hair. He introduced himself to Christina and then sat down. The inspector then said, ", "Okay let us begin with a description of the woman." Christina replied, "oh she had an American accent, she was about five foot eight in height, she inflicted the injuries to my husband, she hit him over the head with a large vase. The colour of hair, jet black, her eyes were green, and she wore blue jeans and a red top. I remember thinking she was doing all the shouting as if she was giving out the orders."

The inspector spoke in a deep voice, "I see, what about the other person?" Christina replied, "He had scars on his forehead, he was about five foot seven, he wore dark jeans and a blue and green top, and he was

American." The inspector gazed into her eyes and said, "You seem pretty sure they were Americans." Christina replied, "Yes, wait there, I just remembered, before my son was kidnapped let me start from the beginning, are you aware of my son's psychic abilities?"

The inspector replied, "Yes I have read of your son's special powers." Christina took a deep breath and continued talking, "My son had a dream that two people were coming from America to kidnap him, and with it only being a dream I didn't act on it, my son's friend, Pepe and his family were about to be thrown out on the street as his father had lost his job, my son said, " he would help them by predicting the EuroMillions lottery numbers and handing them a piece of paper with the winning numbers on it."

inspector Francis became more and more intrigued, he then spoke in a heightened voice, "Go on what happened next?" Christina replied, "Well my husband found out about it and took the piece of paper off David, later on, Pepe and his father, Charles came round for the piece of paper, when Gerald said, "they couldn't have it Charles became angry, Gerald closed the door on them. Charles became mad, he banged on the door several times and then left."

inspector Francis looked into Christina's eyes and said, "They were convinced your son could make this prediction against all odds?" Christina replied, "Yes my husband later turned on the television to watch the results, David predicted all seven numbers, the jackpot was eighty million."

Inspector Francis could not believe his ears, he then spoke in a deep voice, "My God! Imagine if you had placed those numbers on the EuroMillions's jackpot you would have been rich, what I can't understand is you are not the slightest bit bothered, I find this quite strange."

Christina shook her head and replied, "Money isn't everything." The inspector replied, "Yes but it certainly helps, okay what happened next?" Christina replied, "Oh we were celebrating the fact that our son had just picked out all seven jackpot numbers, suddenly a knock on the door, Gerald answered it, stood before him two men in black, one of them said, " he wanted to speak to us about David. My husband was not thinking straight when one of the agents asked what we had been celebrating he mentioned that my son had predicted all seven numbers and the jackpot was eighty million, and then he mentioned that we never even put the numbers on. The agent said, he felt sick, his face turned pale and they just left."

Inspector Francis was now getting a clear picture, he then said, "I believe they came here to try and collect data on your boy, I wonder if somehow these agents are implicated in your son's kidnapping. Two agents, I believe we need to track them down are they are still here in Paris?" The inspector turned to Sergeant Canter and said, ", "Make some enquiries straight away, I believe these agents are the key to this case."

The Sergeant left the room to make further enquiries. the Inspector then turned to Christina and said, "So Christina, the two men calling themselves agents may have not been agents, is that possible?" Christina replied, "I remember my husband saying they were dressed in dark tailored suits and wore shades." The Inspector replied, "Sounds like the CIA, do you think your son could duplicate his win maybe elsewhere, for example, America? They have mega jackpots there; imagine the wealth he could provide. I do not like saying this but to the greedy, your son could be a goldmine, I only wish he was my son and I would be relaxing in the Caribbean without a care in the world. Money, Christina makes the world go round. I will find these American agents and return your son safe and sound of this I promise."

Back at the hotel Harry and Ryan had just finished off a couple of cheeseburgers. Ryan turned to Harry and said, ", "Another beer?" Harry smiled and replied, "Yes, why not?" Ryan handed an ice-cold beer to Harry, he placed it on the table and then spoke in a deep voice, "Do you remember that buddy you used to knock about with when you first joined the CIA? Oh, what was his name? Oh, I remember, Conrad Conspiracy, he said, JFK'S assassination was down to us, the twin towers also us."

Ryan nodded and said, "Yeah, he did start to lose it a bit." Harry shook his head and replied, "A bit! The guy thought I was the antichrist, my God, no wonder his poor mother had him sectioned, he was a regular fruit cake was he not?" Ryan replied, "I remember you used to shout at him a lot."

Harry had a drink of beer then said, "Yeah maybe I did, but he was so annoying, remember afterwards I said, you should choose your friends more wisely do you agree?" Ryan replied, "It's a good thing I am no friend of yours then." Harry erupted like a volcano he shouted, "You What?"

Ryan laughed and replied, "Only joking." Harry put on a funny face and then said, "Oh that's alright." then Ryan gazed into Harry's eyes and said, "Okay let's talk about some of your past friends, remember that tall English lady you met in Texas? Oh, what was her name? Oh, now I remember, Paula the woodpecker, or was it, Paul? She had one hell of a beak on her she reminded me of that kid's show, Sesame Street, Big Bird, that was her nickname wasn't it?"

Harry shook his head and then replied, "That's right, Ryan she was big and yellow, I mentioned engagement and she flew off." Ryan laughed and then said, "Didn't she once take you to London to meet her parents?" Harry took a deep breath and then replied, "Yeah, she was a posh cockney, she had a strange attitude believing she was better than everyone else, her parents where complete snobs, I just didn't fit in, I couldn't speak that stupid false Southern accent. They were all so false."

Ryan laughed and said, "Did you meet the Queen or any members of the Royal family whilst you where there?" Harry replied, "No, I got sick of London, so I travelled to a better city." Ryan smiled and then said, "Which one?" Harry replied, "Liverpool, the birthplace of the Beatles. I sat in the Cavern Club drinking an ice-cold beer, unlike London the people where so warm and friendly, I met a couple of cool guys, Unite Union reps, David and Rollo, they explained to me all about their roles in helping their members overcome injustices in the workplace, of which there was plenty."

Ryan sipped his beer then said, "I must admit Liverpool is one place I would love to visit, did you see any of the Beatles whilst you were there?" Harry shook his head and then replied, "No, I did watch a Beatles cover group, I love that song, 'The long and winding road'." Ryan itched his nose then said, "My favourite hit by the Beatles has to be, 'Hey Dude'." Harry suddenly broke out into laughter, he shook his head and then replied, "Hey Dude! it was 'Hey Jude', not dude. I reckon John Lennon was my favourite Beatle, such an amazing voice, poor guy came over to our country and was wasted because he believed in peace, killed because he campaigned against weapons of mass destruction. The guy that did it was brain washed into pulling the trigger."

Ryan agreed with a slow nod of his head, a brief silence Ryan then said, "Okay, so big bird flew off, who was your next victim? Oh, I remember, Pathological Pixie, she slashed your tyres with a flick knife, my, you pick some mad ones didn't you have her locked up?"

Harry replied, "Yeah, she was one bad bitch, still her cooking was heaven." Ryan laughed and said, "You're confused, it was hell, you were always ill, she used to lace your food with rat poison." Harry shook his head and replied, "Cheers for reminding me." Ryan laughed and said, "Okay anytime, anyway, the point I was trying to get over is we are both poor judges of characters."

Harry took a deep breath and agreed with Ryan. All of a sudden, Harry's mobile rang out. Harry turned to Ryan and said, "I hope this isn't mad Mellor." He then answered the call, his worst nightmare, it was an angry chief Mellor, he shouted, ", "This is Chief Mellor, the kid has been kidnapped, you were supposed to be watching over him, find out what is happening, stay for one more day and then get back to my office, you and your sidekick expect to get your balls busted. Now go over and get information do I make myself clear?"

Harry replied, "straight away, he then hung up. Ryan shook his head and then spoke in a concerned voice, "What did he say?" Harry replied, "Looks like we got to go to the scene of the crime and gather information, then thank God we are leaving this place."

The Inspector had finished interviewing Christina and had arranged a car to take her to the hospital to be with her husband. The Inspector then returned to the scene of the crime, he arrived just after Harry and Ryan, as they walked over to the house, the inspector parked up quickly and then rushed towards the two men dressed in black suits, he the then shouted, "Hey you two

Americans?" Harry turned around and looked the Inspector in the eyes and replied, "Are you talking to us?" The Inspector nodded and said, "Yes." he then produced his badge and spoke in a deep voice, "My name is inspector Francis." Harry looked at the card. The inspector then said, "I want you both to accompany me to the Police station to answer some questions."

Harry laughed and replied, "Okay we know who you are, but you don't know who we are." the Inspector replied, "I have reason to believe you are a couple of CIA agents am I not correct?" Ryan laughed and said, "Harry you got to hand it to this guy he is a genius." Harry shook his head and said, "why the hell should we cooperate with you?" The inspector replied, "Look we can do this the easy way or the hard way I could have several officers handcuff you and take you to the station."

Harry looked to the ground for a brief second and then he gazed into the Inspector's eyes and said, "No, you're right Inspector, a crime has been committed and everyone is a suspect, after all, we are on your soil." The Inspector pointed to the hire car and said, "Over there is your hire car, I want you to get in it and follow me to the station, remember the innocent have nothing to hide." Harry smiled and replied, "Okay you got yourself a deal, we will follow you to the station."

Harry turned to Ryan and said, "Come on let's go." They both walked towards the hire car, Harry yawned then scratched his head, he then spoke in a low voice,

"Oh what a smart arse that guy is he's so irritating I hate the French." Ryan agreed as they got into the car and followed the Inspector back to the station. Harry turned to Ryan as they arrived at the Police station and said, ", "When we get there I will call the Chief, let's see what he has to say on this matter, he will have us out of there in minutes can't wait to see the French guy's face."

Harry pulled over into the police station car park, the Inspector got out of his car followed by Harry and Ryan. The Inspector turned his attention to Harry and smiled, as they all walked into the station Harry laughed at the inspector and then said, "I need to make a phone call is that okay?"

Francis smiled and replied, "I anticipated you would try to pull that one, I have spoken with Chief Mellor, he doesn't want any diplomatic incidents between our two countries, he wants you both to cooperate or face the consequences, do I make myself clear?"

Harry gritted his teeth trying to control his anger and then he lost and said, ", "Control, who the hell do you think you are talking to? I am an American CIA agent, if it wasn't for my country winning the war you would all be a nation of sausage eaters talking German."

The inspector could not believe his ears, he took a deep breath and spoke, I do not like your tone I know all about your mission as I have spoken, with Chief Mellor. I will now call him again and inform him of your hostile attitude, you mad Americans think you are above Europe, well I disagree."

Ryan began to panic, he turned to the Inspector and said, "No need to call the Chief we will cooperate won't we Harry? Look, Harry, get a grip on yourself, calm down." Harry nodded his head.

The inspector then said, ", "I need you both to follow me to the interview room I want to interview you one by one, the pair of you to tell the truth about the day you visited David's house. First, I will interview you, Ryan. Harry please wait inside the waiting room and help yourself to coffee." Harry snarled and then turned and entered the restroom. inspector Francis smiled at Ryan and said, ", your friend, Harry, he is such a hot head how do you manage to work with him as a partner?"

Ryan replied, "Oh you sort of get used to his hot-headed ways." Ryan mustered a confident smile as they both entered the interview room, the Inspector then said, "Right I would like to introduce you to Sergeant Canter, he is here to simply make notes, he is to be my note-taker, right Ryan sit here opposite me."

Ryan sat down opposite the Inspector. "Your Chief informed me you and your partner were sent to Paris on a sort of mission, you wanted to check to see if the intelligence on the boy was correct, your country wanted a piece of the action so to speak. CIA serves the nation's interest by collecting and analyzing foreign intelligence related to National security threats, you travel around the world trying to convince everyone to share secrets with the U.S Government and have undercover skills and are experts at telling lies, is all of this correct ?"

Ryan smiled and then replied, "That is so correct." The inspector smiled and then said, "I thought so, you read a file on David, your job was to visit David and his family and somehow persuade them into leaving France and move to America where you could take advantage of David and use his remarkable abilities for your own means."

Ryan grinned at the inspector and then gazed into his eyes, Ryan then replied, "Okay Francis you know everything." The inspector then said, ", "Good now tell me something I don't know, tell me what happened when you visited the house to talk to the Family?" Ryan replied, "Oh where shall I begin my friend? Harry wasn't feeling well." The inspector then spoke with a raised voice, "I know he had a virus, you brought some drugs from a store, you spoke to the lady behind the counter telling her your friend, Harry was bedridden, a very good alibi was it not?"

All of a sudden Ryan felt speechless. Francis looked into Ryan's eyes and said, "You have gone quiet why the sudden silence?" Ryan shook his head then spoke in a calm voice, "I don't know what to say, you seem to be making out we are guilty of a crime." The inspector replied, "Talk to me, persuade me of your innocence, what happened when Harry spoke to Gerald? I believe you are the quiet one, your partner does all the talking, you, my friend just listen."

Ryan smiled and said, "Not always, Harry talks very fast sometimes I can't keep up, I don't always hear what he's saying." The inspector scratched the back of his head and then spoke in a quiet voice, "Alright what did you hear him say?" Ryan replied, "I heard Harry tell Gerald about us being a couple of government agents." "So, he did not mention which government, he never said you were a couple of CIA agents?" Ryan replied, "Sorry I can't remember you will have to ask Harry."

The inspector shook his head and replied, "don't worry I will. what else did Harry say?" Ryan replied, "listen to me, Francis I never heard what he said, ask Harry."

the inspector gazed into Ryan's contemptuous eyes and then spoke in a raised voice, "you both heard the noise of celebration from the household did you not? Gerald was not thinking straight he informed Harry about his son predicting all seven numbers on the EuroMillions, he then informed Harry about the jackpot prize eighty million Euros and the fact they never entered these numbers into the draw because they did not need the money. this is when your partner was struck down with a mystery virus, I am correct am I not?"

Ryan replied, "no he complained about feeling sick a couple of hours before we arrived." the inspector then said, "so you still went ahead with your operation even though your partner was sick?" Ryan replied, with a raised voice, "I know you don't believe me but that is what actually happened, Chief Mellor was busting our balls, especially mine, he said he was going to demote me to a beat cop in the roughest neighbourhood in Washington DC."

the inspector smiled and said, "yes I can see he puts the fear of God into you, yes it must have been hard for you. that will be all I have finished with you go and ask your friend Harry to come in he is next."

Ryan stood up relieved his ordeal was over, he knew he had done himself proud. Ryan walked out with his head held high. He approached Harry with a wide smile he then spoke, "Everything is fine I did us proud." Harry stood up and smiled to himself, his confidence slowly returned all the time a voice inside his head was saying, "play it cool play it cool."

He knocked and they slowly entered the room, the inspector's voice echoed all around the room "Come in Harry take a seat did you have a coffee?" Harry replied, "yes several." the inspector smiled and said, "Oh how I like your American sense of humour." Harry produced a cool contemptuous smile and then sat down the room.

Sergeant Canter sat quietly taking notes. Francis gazed into Harry's eyes and then spoke in a heightened voice, "I am sorry to hear about your illness, Ryan informed me it all started after a conversation with David's father Gerald." Harry laughed out loud and the replied, "He never said anything of the sort, we both know the sickness started a couple of hours before we arrived." the inspector laughed and then said, "Good, congratulations are in order you have both got your stories straight that only arouses suspicion in my eyes."

Harry shook his head in disbelief, he then spoke in a raised voice, "but you've got French eyes I wouldn't expect any different from you." the inspector could not believe his ears, he then spoke with a firm voice, "You are supposed to be a cool CIA agent, the comment you have just made is very offensive even racist. The next time you make a comment like that I shall have you arrested do I make myself clear?"

Harry replied, "Crystal clear, No more insulting comments." the inspector turned to the Sergeant and said, "make a note Sergeant, Harry finds racist comments funny." anxiety twisted Harry's face suddenly his anger rose he then shouted, "Good god damn you!" his mind began to whisper "stay cool stay cool." the inspector began to smile, Harry cooled down and then he spoke in a calm voice, "I didn't mean that I am really a nice guy I guess we just got off on the wrong foot, you just got me all wrong."

the inspector smiled once more and the said, "Harry my friend the big American complex Washington D.C what a dump." Harry knew the inspector was trying to provoke him. Harry swallowed his pride then laughed he then said, "you're right Francis, Washington D.C is a dump did you know Pope Francis visits this year ?" the inspector nodded his head and then replied, "yes, I will be visiting looking for a missing teenager, your Chief Mellor is a good man, I wanted more information about you and he said, " no. you have your alibi everything ties up you are free to go."

Harry smiled then stood up, he then said, "I would like to shake your hand and apologise for my stupid behaviour." Harry shook the Inspector's hand, he then turned round and left the room, he walked over to Ryan. the Inspector turned to the Sergeant and said, ", "arrange for a tail on them I believe their next move will be to leave France as soon as possible, I will follow them back to Washington D.C., I believe they will lead me to David."

Harry smiled and shook Ryan's hand he then said, "let's get the hell out of here." Harry and Ryan walked out of the police station believing the victory was all theirs. Inspector Francis walked over to the laboratory, an officer handed in the results from the fingerprint match, the Inspector said, ", "now what do we have here?" the inspector read out the results out loud as Sergeant Canter joined him in the forensic laboratory. "Very good Canter, we have two matches, we are looking for two Americans male and female the male is called Peter Smith the female Daisy, I believe David has been kidnapped and taken to Washington D.C., the same place our couple of agents are from. Sergeant we shall leave for Washington D.C immediately, that is where is David is being kept hostage. I believe he is being kept because he can predict numbers, that kid could use his powers to make a lot of money in Washington D.C."

The Sergeant said, "I must admit I watch a lot of American movies; the CIA is always made out to be special what are your views?" The inspector smiled and replied, "this is real life, not a movie."

Daisy and Peter were now hiding in an old disused

warehouse, David was locked in a dark damp room, he sat in silence gazing at every shadow, the floor was cold. David closed his eyes praying for light a couple of minutes later out of the darkness his mind whispered "has Cavoc come to me?" to anxious silence then communication, David listened to a softly spoken voice, "David do not be afraid I am a messenger on behalf of Cavoc, he asked me to visit you in the New World."

David could feel pure warmth, the light became brighter and brighter David began to blink and frown and then David slowly opened his eyes stood before him, an Angel. he was mesmerised by her beauty and perfection the light she radiated completely lit up the room, once more she spoke in a soft peaceful relaxing voice, "my message to you is pure and simple, good will conquer over evil, a Saint by the name of Francis will leave France, he will help you gain the freedom you so desire."

David felt a sense of relief, he then smiled gazing into the angel's emerald green eyes David then thanked the angel for her words of wisdom "Thank you for bringing me hope in my hour of darkness". All of a sudden, the lock on the door opened as the angel disappeared and the darkness returned.

Daisy appeared from the shadows complete with a torch, she shone the light into David's eyes and said, "Hey kid, I heard you talking to someone who was it?" David smiled and replied, "Would you believe me if I said, "it was an angel?" Daisy looked to David her face was full of annoyance, she then spoke with a raised voice, "you think you are so smart compared to us, don't you?" David grinned he then replied with newfound confidence "yes I do". Daisy then said, "kid don't push your luck! anyway, I got some news about your mother and father, let's do a deal exchange information".

David gazed into her wild sinister eyes and said, "What information?" Daisy laughed and replied, "why did those bad CIA agents ask us to kidnap you, what value are you to them?" David replied without thinking, "oh I can predict the future, as we speak Saint Francis is travelling from France to find me, justice will prevail."

Daisy then spoke in a soft voice, "Yeah right kid, Harry the CIA agent is going to pay us one million for kidnapping you tell me why" David replied, "why, that's not much cash for me, he's underpaying you." Daisy's face became twisted with anxiety with a shade of impatience in her voice as she spoke, "what the hell do you mean kid?" Daisy's eyes suddenly lit up, "tell me kid what are you really worth?" David smiled and replied, "the light in here is terrible."

Daisy let out a wailing scream, her anger erupted like a volcano, she shouted out Peter's name. Peter started to panic, he rushed into the room and said, "What's the matter, honey?" Daisy replied, "shut it just do as you are told." bring David the big flashlight." David smiled for once he was in control he then said, "I could do with a drink the damp smell in here leaves my mouth dry."

Daisy then shouted, "Peter get the kid something to eat and drink and make it snappy." Peter stopped and looked to Daisy in confusion, Daisy spoke once more with a raised voice, "what you "What are you doing dumb ass? do as the kid says, is that alright?" David replied, "well I suppose so." Daisy Smiled and said, "alright dear David let's get back to our little conversation how much are you really worth?" David replied, "well Harry, appeared at my house just after I predicted the numbers for EuroMillions, the jackpot was eighty million."

Daisy took a deep breath; she saw dollar signs before her eyes. Peter entered the room with the flashlight and bottle of water he handed them to David and said, "here son a nice drink." Daisy then said, "Listen, Peter and listen closely, David tell uncle Peter what you have just told me." David replied, "well, Harry appeared at my house the evening I predicted all seven numbers on the EuroMillions, the jackpot was eighty million."

Peter looked into David's eyes and spoke, "so kid your parents are rich and Harry wants a piece of the action?" David replied, "no we didn't place the numbers on." Daisy then said, "wait I bet you have special powers to predict winning numbers is that correct? I know what that crafty son of a bitch was up to something, imagine if David predicted the winning numbers of the American lottery."

Peter thinks for a minute and then replies, "my god that could be up to two hundred million dollars." Daisy shakes her head in disbelief she then said, "Harry that lousy bastard was only going to give me one million and we took all the risks." David laughed out loud and said, "you're both right he's played you for a right couple of fools."

Daisy gazed at David's eyes and said, "don't push it, kid, oh I mean I am sorry our lottery numbers are only six numbers." David now spoke with greater confidence, "if you looked after me this could be easily achieved." Peter became excited he the said, "my God Daisy did you hear what the kid just said? we're rich." Daisy smiled and said, " David I believe you are an angel come down to Earth to reward me and Peter because of our poor childhoods did you know we were both abused? sorry, David, I seem to be getting carried away, oh your parents are just fine they are just awaiting your release as soon as you help us win a little money we can let you go back home to beautiful France. such a lovely place is it not Peter?"

Suddenly she had an idea and said, "the lottery isn't till the end of the week maybe we should test his powers with a little horse racing bet if that's ok with you." David replied, "yes, I now have light and water, but no food." Peter then produced a candy bar and then handed it to David. Peter and Daisy then walked out of the room closing and locking the door behind them.

Daisy reached into her bag; she was wild-eyed with a look of malice. Daisy pulled out a semi-automatic pistol, she then looked to Peter and said, "oh Peter what is this is it?" Peter replied, "a semi-automatic pistol of course." Daisy then said, "okay who am I?" Peter replied, "why you're Daisy a regular pistol-packing flower." Daisy then spoke with a raised voice, "well then remember not to piss me off, what we need is more firepower in case the chuckle brothers turn up what you reckon?" Peter replied, "how about Macko I have got his number?" Daisy became even more wide-eyed she then replied, ", "machine gun Macko, now there is a real homicidal maniac, good, give him a call I have someone in mind bad Boris from the Caribbean."

Peter scratched his head then spoke, "he is really bad are you sure?" Daisy replied, "the worse the better, remember we still got some of Harry's money, imagine if one of them could place some bets for us and no one would be the wiser, a run-up to the big one what you reckon?" Peter replied, "yeah that's a smart move Daisy the key is to keep the kid happy what about the chuckle brothers they have to find us first if they turn up, we shoot them dead."

Peter then gave Macko a call and said, "do you fancy making some serious money? we just need some protection, bring your bag of weapons with you." Macko agreed, Peter then hung up. Daisy called Boris, she got the same response, money is hard to come by and so are jobs that make you rich, he also agreed.

back in Paris, Harry looks to Ryan and said, "look I got to call Chief Mellor is that okay?" Ryan replied, "he's going to be so pissed off can't we go in and see him after we have got the flight home?" Harry replied, "no let's do things my way."

Harry sat down and picked up his mobile and called the Chief. He was filled with rage he shouted, "you pair get back to Washington D.C on the double do I make myself clear? did you cooperate with Inspector Francis?" Harry replied, " yes sir we did we even shook hands." the Chief then said, " the whole operation was a complete waste of taxpayers' money, a complete fuck-up, get the next flight home I want two written reports on my desk as soon as possible, do I make myself clear?" Harry replied, "yes sir see you soon."

Harry then hung up. Ryan looked to Harry panic fears fluttered his mind he then said, "what did Mellor say?" Harry replied, "Mellor the Muppet God I hate that guy, you hate him as, well don't you?" Ryan replied, "yeah so what did he say? the usual, let me guess he wants two written reports on our fuck-ups as soon as possible so he is really pissed?"

Harry replied, "I reckon so let's get out of here and get back to the good old U.S.A." Ryan then said, "hadn't you better contact the delightful Daisy I got a bad feeling about her she's so unpredictable." Harry agreed nodding his head he then said, "yeah you're right that makes the two of us if she finds out about the kid's psychic gifts, she will take advantage of him."

Harry then made a call to Daisy, she sat next to Peter listening to her phone ringing out loud she smiled and turned to Peter and said, "I bet you this is Harry." Daisy slowly picked up her phone and answered it, Harry began speaking in an angry voice, "you know who this is? It's me, is the kid safe and sound "? Daisy replied, "yes, he's such a lovely kid me and Peter are thinking of adoption, he reminds me of an angel." Harry with a raised voice said, "look, stop messing around I haven't got time for this, where you keeping him?"

Daisy laughed then turned off her phone. Harry grew hysterical and began screaming like a madman, "the damn bitch knows, she's just hung up on me." Harry punched the door in a fit of anger, Ryan tried to stay calm he then said, "you know the bitch, what will be her next move?"

Harry replied, " she knows I will eventually find her, my guess she will bring others into the deal as back up ready for when we show up, I must need my head testing hiring her for the kidnapping, it's a mistake that will make me rich or dead."

Ryan rubbed his eyes the said, "Harry now she knows about the kid she will fight to the death to keep him, won't she?" Harry replied, "remember after we split up, she got a tattoo done on the back of a semi-automatic pistol above it the words 'Daisy the pistol-packing flower' what a homicidal bitch. whatever did I see in her?"

Ryan replied, "an easy lay hey Harry?" Harry pushed Ryan and replied, "why you cheeky good for nothing." Harry laughed, then Ryan did the same. Harry then said, "maybe that's all she was, after my divorce I was kinda lonely do you know what I mean?" Ryan replied, "Harry the kind of word you're looking for is desperate, that's why we are in a mess is it not?"

Harry replied, "now wait a minute at present we are in the clear, does the report state that I feel somewhat responsible for the kidnapping of the kid instead of suffering from a virus no it does not. let's get back now, on the way I'll think of a few more words to add to that. This Inspector Francis ain't no fool, did you know he has had two of his men following us?"

Ryan replied, "no Harry I had no idea, what we going to do about that bitch Daisy and pathetic Peter?" "We, my friend, are going to hunt them down like the dogs that they are. When we find them, I want us to adopt a strict new rule, shoot to kill. now my friend let us leave and get on a flight back to the wonderful Washington D. C.

Back in Washington D.C., David shone his flashlight into a dark corner of the room, panic fears fluttered his mind, there before his eyes several cockroaches moving back and forward. David was not accustomed to such a horrible sight; he began to shout out loud his heart was pounding. The sound of David's cries echoed all around the warehouse. Peter jumped out of his seat and raced towards the door he then with great haste opened the lock he then raced inside to find out what the problem was.

David shone the flashlight at the cockroaches "look at them horrible creatures." Peter laughed and said, "never saw a cockroach before you're too posh for us kid". Peter removed his shoe and began to kill each and every one of the cockroaches, he then put his shoe back on. he then said, "Okay kid they're all dead, you hungry? got some cold beans going spare."

David shook his head and replied, "No thank you I just lost my appetite." Peter then reached inside his pocket and the produced another candy bar, "do you prefer that?" David replied, "yes anything's better than cold beans." Peter laughed as he handed David the candy bar, he then left locking the door behind him.

Daisy had just finished off her cold beans, she looked to Peter with a fixed expression and said, "what the hell was the problem?" Peter replied, "oh cockroaches it's alright I killed them all." Daisy smiled and said, "let's hope you have that killer instinct when the two big cockroaches appear.

suddenly there was a loud knock on the door which echoed all around the warehouse. Daisy shook her head and said, "Peter don't panic pass me the pistol I will check it out it's probably Macko."

Peter handed the pistol to Daisy she then opened the door slowly standing before her was Macko larger than life he spoke in a deep voice, " Hi it's me, Macko you must be Daisy, I am a friend of Peter, I brought the bag of weapons like he asked." Daisy smiled and said, "good welcome to my humble abode."

Daisy looked Macko up and down and said, "my God you are a fine figure of a man." Macko stood six feet five a giant imposing man he had tattoos embroidered across his body and massive biceps and bulged shoulders. he had Hispanic blood running through his veins, he was rough and ready. Macko lived by the code of the bullet.

Peter walked over to Macko and said, "hi Macko long time no see, what you been doing lately?" Macko replied, "oh the usual stuff, a kill here a kill there." Peter grinned then said, "good, so you haven't changed?" Macko replied, "no I will never change and never stop until someone fills me full of lead."

Peter then said, "haven't you been shot before?" Macko replied, "yeah it goes with the territory. anyway, I brought the bag of guns and something extra, four bottles of Jack Daniel's."

Peter and Macko embraced Peter then said, "let us celebrate." Daisy laughed and then said, "this way gentlemen, the bar is this way." Macko looked to Peter in disbelief and said, "what you got a bar?" Peter and Daisy laughed out loud Peter then replied, "Macko my friend, ignore Daisy she just has a wicked sense of humour."

Macko shook his head laughing. they all sat down as Macko placed his bag on an old table he then opened it up and handed Peter and Daisy a bottle each. they then sat reminiscing about the good old days, all of a sudden there was another loud knock on the door. Daisy smiled placing her bottle of Jack Daniel's on the table. "that must be Boris I will get the door; you boys carry on drinking."

Daisy picked up her semi-automatic pistol just in case it wasn't Boris, she opened the door slowly standing before her was big bad Boris, king of the Caribbean, a big warm smile and then she spoke, " hi Boris how are you doing? it's been a while but it's nice to see your big warm smile."

Boris replied, "you is a poet Daisy I know you are just a bit crazy." Daisy laughed out loud and then said, "nothing has changed there then." Boris then broke out into a song "Daisy, Daisy you is driving me crazy, you're so much fun when you got your gun a pistol-packing flower that grows on me by the hour, you look so fine won't you be mine ?"

Daisy smiled and replied, "Boris what about Peter?" Boris replied, "let's make some money and run away together back to my hometown, we could be the king and queen of the Caribbean."

Boris was six feet three inches a solidly built man complete with dreadlocks and a Bob Marley T-shirt. Boris had a reputation for violence and homicide, he would shoot anyone for money. he had a burning desire to return to the Caribbean a rich man.

Daisy then said, "oh Boris we will have to see at present I am with Peter." Boris then changed the subject to his one true love he then said, "you mentioned money on the telephone, Sister how much money is we talking?" Daisy replied, "you haven't changed straight to the point. look big fellow I aim to make you rich and you will be the king of the Caribbean."

Boris smiled and then said, "good Sister you are talking my kind of language I am still one badass ghetto assassin if you know what I mean." Daisy replied, "good that's why I picked you for your reputation, it proceeds you, the Caribbean killer. how many men have you killed?" Boris replied, "believe it or not thirteen, what you reckon?" Daisy replied, "my, that's unlucky but I know how we can improve that score, I have a couple of knuckleheads that need wasting."

Boris gazed into the Warehouse and said, "is it those two over there?" Daisy shook her head and then replied, "no they're friends okay, I better introduce you." Boris shut the door and then walked over with Daisy to the table. Macko and Peter were drinking their Jack Daniel's, Daisy then said, "right Boris I want you to meet my fellow, Peter and his mate, machine gun Macko." Boris then spoke in a raised voice, "it's nice to meet you both my name is Boris king of the Caribbean, I have heard of machine gun Macko, I see you have brought your bag of goodies."

Macko gazed at his holdall filled with weapons, they all shook hands, Daisy then handed Boris a bottle of Jack Daniel's, the abandoned warehouse had old beds and mattresses a table and several chairs complete with a damp smell. they all sat around exchanging stories of their homicidal past. very soon it started to go dark, Daisy lit several candles. Peter turned to Macko and said, "did you bring with you food and cola?" Macko replied, "yes it's in my holdall."

Macko opened up his holdall and then reached inside and pulled out a bag, he then emptied contents of the bag onto the table three bottles of Coca-Cola and several sealed batches. Boris smiled and said, "food man I haven't eaten for hours." Peter laughed and said, "help yourselves to the food." Peter picked up a batch and a bottle of cola and said, "these are for the kid." Boris looked shocked panic fears fluttered his mind he then spoke in confusion, "what kid?" Macko also looked to Peter then replied, "oh the kid that's going to make us all rich. oh, Macko, another thing did you bring the racing paper for the evening's races?" Macko replied, "yes I got it here."

Boris shook with impatience; he felt a red mist descending. Daisy read the situation and responded accordingly she then spoke in a firm voice, "Peter answer our friend's question." "oh, sorry Boris we got a kid that has amazing powers, he can predict future betting results." Boris shook his head in disbelief he then said, "man, do not insult my intelligence." Peter kept his cool and replied, "Okay my friend, tell me how much money you would like in the next twenty-four hours?"

Boris wiped away the perspiration from his forehead he then replied, "Okay man I would like five thousand dollars, you got twenty-four hours?" Peter mustered a confident smile as Macko handed Peter the racing paper. Peter then spoke, in a loud voice, "alright everybody it's time to get the kid to weave his magic."

Peter stood up and then walked over to the room in which David was locked in. He slowly opened the door; David was fast asleep on an old bed. Peter shook David's shoulder and said, "wake up kid wake up" David opened his eyes slowly he then yawned. "I see you still got that flashlight on; the battery is fading what you going to do when the battery runs out?" David yawned once more and then spoke, "oh I am sure you will get me a new one." Peter replied, "yeah kid, let me light some candles for now."

Peter produced some candles and lit them straight away, placing them on a small table. Peter then said, "kid you got to do something for me, oh here look what I brought you a fresh batch with chicken on it and a bottle of Coca-Cola." Peter placed them also on the table he then said, "I said I would look after you, didn't I?" David replied, "yes what's the catch?" "you're the catch kid, you are the catch here, I got you a racing paper and a pen all you have to do pick out some winners for uncle Peter." David replied, "but you're not my uncle, are you?" Peter replied, "Okay smartass, just pick out the winners and I'll get you anything you require."

David then spoke in a quiet voice, "oh alright then, I want an American burger with fries." Peter agreed, then handed the racing paper to David and said, "Look kid these are the races different times and different odds here is a pen just put a circle around the winning horses can you do it?"

David replied, "Okay I need concentration, just stand outside for a minute." Peter smiled and then said, "Good kid I know you can do it, remember the more the merrier." Peter left David in peace for a minute whilst he picked out various horses in different races. Peter returned with a confident smile on his face he then spoke, "okay kid, you circled out the winners how many horses you picked out?" David replied, "oh lucky seven." Peter looked at the horses, he scratched his head then spoke, "My, kid you picked out some outsiders some good odds, I reckon a seven-horse accumulator is in order." Peter smiled, he knew he had no choice he had promised bad Boris five thousand dollars, he had twenty-four hours to deliver or else."

Peter looked into David's eyes and said, "you're not going to let me down they are all winners, aren't they?" David smiled and replied, "don't worry just don't forget my order." Peter replied, "ok kid I won't forget." Peter then left the room locking it behind him. Peter then walked over to Macko and said, "ok the moment of truth here Macko I want you to place this bet it's a seven-horse accumulator, I got three hundred dollars." Boris interrupted gazing into Peter's eyes, he was desperate to make up his total kill to fourteen, he then spoke in a deep voice, "it is finished, the bottle man, I is needing a little sleep."

Peter put on a false smile and said, "okay Boris help yourself to one of those old beds." Boris stood up and proceeded towards the bed of his choice. Peter then turned to Macko and said, "you know what must be done?" Macko replied, "ok but what is my share in the deal?" "You can have five thousand dollars it's not bad for a few day's work." Macko replied, "alright it will do for now. Are you sure this kid will deliver the winners?" Peter replied, "have a little faith." as he handed Macko the money and betting newspaper. Macko smiled and said, "I will leave my holdall here that way you know I will definitely be back." Peter laughed and then spoke in a confident voice, "my friend me and you go back a long way we have our moral code." Macko agreed and then left with the money."

Daisy looked to Peter and said, "my, Peter can you trust that guy?" Peter replied, "listen my little flower, that guy once saved my life did, I tell you the story?" Daisy replied, "no do tell what happened?"

Peter replied, "oh I was amongst the urban community." Daisy laughed and said, "Peter it's the ghetto." Peter then carried on with his story and said, "yeah anyway, I was just an innocent bystander I witnessed this animal shoot dead a yak, yeah she was fat and ugly." he then pointed his gun at me, Macko appeared, he pushed me to one side and took a bullet for me."

Daisy then said, "what happened next?" Peter replied, "oh Macko became very angry, the guy realised he had just put a bullet in Macko, something you just don't do, he had such a bad reputation on the street, the guy was just a rat a gutter punk he began to panic, he turned around and ran. The one thing about Macko is he never misses, he pulled out his machine pistol and filled the guy full of lead, that's how he got his nickname machine gun Macko."

Daisy smiled and then said, "wow Peter that was a great bedtime story, oh well it's been a long day I am going to get me some shut-eye." Peter agreed and they were soon in bed.

Macko made his way towards the bookies, he had no fear walking along the grey tarmac. Macko looked up at the night sky, the stars shone bright livid with wrath. Macko gazed at every shadow, as he walked along the sound of the traffic echoed all around the unforgiving streets.

Macko entered the shop, a few strange looks from the locals, and then he filled in the betting slip. He walked up to the counter and was greeted by an old man who spoke in a strange accent, "Hi Sir what have we here?" Macko handed him the betting slip, he was short and had a very tanned face wrinkled like a walnut he then said, "alright Sir a seven-horse accumulator are you sure about this?" Macko replied, " yeah, here is three hundred dollars, my poor father is on his death bed I promised him I would put the bet on." the betting shop assistant looked up at Macko's auburn complexion, a voice inside his head said, " don't mess with this guy he then said, " I am sorry to hear about your father, you're right we must respect his wishes." He slowly counted out the money, three hundred dollars. The cashier then forgot who he was dealing with he said, " The odds on these races are tough, you sure your poor father would have wanted you to put on such a bet? The odds are stacked against you, I would say impossible odds are you sure?"

Macko gritted his teeth, his livid eyes gazed upon the little man he then spoke with a shade of impatience in his voice, " look put the bet on now understand ?" The little man replied, "Oh sorry Sir it's your money I will put the bet on for you right away."

He quickly processed the bet and placed the money in the till he then said, "thank you, Sir, here is your slip complete with odds." Macko took the slip placing it into his pocket. Macko then left the betting shop and began the journey back to the warehouse.

The following day Harry and Ryan were now back in Washington D.C., Harry climbed out of bed his head confused, perspiration leaking all over his body. He headed for his pride and joy the shower, he turned on the shower, the water was warm. He was soon finished, he took a deep breath and then stepped out of the shower and dried himself with a large towel. He then reached inside a draw and got out his boxer shorts and then slipped them on.

Harry picked up a hairbrush and then moved gingerly towards a place he despised the mirror, he gazed into it his eyes, they looked miserable in their perplexity. He then began to talk to himself in a heightened voice, " shit I've faded to grey what's happened to my face? Its full of wrinkles must be the job if only I could turn back the clock."

Harry lived in a modest one-bedroom apartment, he hated the fact he had served his country for most of his life, had nothing to show for it except for an old Cadillac and a selection of worn-down tailored suits.

Harry finished brushing his hair, he turned away from the dreaded mirror and then suddenly the telephone rang out. After a brief second Harry answered it. "hi Harry, it's me, Ryan, what time you picking me up in your old banger?" Harry replied, "I ain't." Ryan said, "what do you mean you ain't?" Harry replied, "rephrase the banger bit my car has feelings you know." "Okay, Harry what time you are picking me up in your classic Cadillac?" Harry laughed and said, "that's better I shall pick you up in one hour or less is that okay?" Ryan replied, "But Harry, how less half an hour quarter of an hour or what?" Harry replied, "God you're hard work, I know I will pick you up in forty-five minutes." he then hung up.

Ryan looked to his girlfriend, Cindy, she was short, petite and possessed such appealing beauty. He then said, "my God, he always hangs up on me?" Cindy replied, "it's your own fault, why don't you ask for a transfer? You need to get away from horrid Harry, the guy's living in a bygone age, he's a regular walking, talking Dinosaur, isn't he?" Ryan replied, "yeah, I hate to say this but you're right, Harry is well past his sell-by date."

Ryan took a deep breath and then said, " guess I am stuck in a rut I've been with Harry for far too long." Cindy shook her head then spoke in a low voice, " does he talk about me I know he can be so patronising ?" Ryan replied, "Harry likes you; he says you're a regular Cindy doll."

Harry found himself again looking into the mirror and talking to himself. "I suppose shit happens we all get old, even the good-looking ones like me." Harry began to cough he then said to himself "God I need some fresh air."

Harry turned around and made his way to the window, he opened it slowly allowing a cool breeze to enter his rented apartment, he then listened to the sounds of the neighbourhood people shouting and arguing about whose turn it was to do the school run, the sounds of Car horns echoed all around the apartment.

Harry shook his head with a sense of compulsion, he then closed his window with a bang. Harry walked over to his television, he grabbed tight hold of his control and then proceeded to flick through the channels until he reached the news. His mind whispered "what more bad news? War global warming, death and decay. He thought "shit life's a bitch."

Harry turned off his television and then decided to make himself a coffee. He made it strong adding spoons of sugar just the way he liked it. Harry took a sip and then got dressed, he opened his wardrobe gazing at his selection of tailored suits. Harry picked out his favourite suit and then slowly got dressed. Harry then slipped into his well-polished shoes and then the following final touch, his designer shades.

Memories of Daisy flooded back, flashbacks of the times they had together, the good and the bad. He knew he would have to kill her to shut her up. Suddenly his mind cried out "God damn you what have you done?" Harry picked up his automatic pistol and pretended to shoot the mirror. "God, I hate you mirror"

Harry placed his pistol back into his holster and then proceeded to make his way out of the apartment. He stopped outside and looked up, gazing at the strange cloud formations, a cool breeze left trees and shrubs moving to and fro.

Harry walked over to his Cadillac he opened the door and climbed inside. This was his pride and joy, his only true friend. Harry put the key into the ignition, his motor was very reliable and started first time. Harry pulled off slowly towards Ryan's place. It wasn't that far, very soon he was sitting outside Ryan's house.

Harry was very impatient; his hands began to shake and then he took a deep breath. Harry was really pissed, he opened his car door he felt a red mist descending, a sinister Hispanic male appeared walking towards Harry. He looked at Harry and then his Cadillac. Harry's anger erupted like a volcano he began to lose control he shouted, "what the fuck are you looking at?" The man looked at Harry in total confusion, he wore a cap and a designer T-shirt, he was of average height and build and his eyes were filled with fear.

He reached inside his pocket, but Harry with lightning reflexes pulled out his Glock semi-automatic pistol and pointed it at the Hispanic male. He then said, "you clown, do you know who I am? Raise your hands high in the air."

Ryan stepped out of his front door and pointed to Harry. "My God! What is that madman doing?" Cindy replied, "that guy is going to get you both killed Ryan replied, "Look Cindy Harry's been my partner for years I know how he ticks I will go over there and take control of the situation."

Ryan kissed Cindy and said, "don't worry I'll sort this." Ryan proceeded towards Harry, his mind whispered, "shit, is Harry losing it?"

A Hispanic lady and a child appeared, she walked into the line of fire. Harry looked on in disbelief as the Hispanic male with the cap dropped his hands the lady reached inside his pocket and produced a candy bar. Harry lowered his pistol, a voice in his mind kept repeating itself, Harry banged the top of his car.

Ryan looked into Harry's wild livid eyes. and said, "shit what's going on Harry? You just pulled a gun on the guy from the local candy store." Harry shook his head and said, "I know I pulled out my pistol on him before he could pull out his candy bar, anyway that guy was eyeballing me and my motor, we both have feelings you know. Anyway, you make me crazy every time I come to your house to pick up, you're never ready. I saw Sindy doll from the corner of my eye, she was slagging me off, wasn't she?" Ryan replied, "well Harry what do you expect? your behaviour isn't strictly rational is it?"

Harry put away his pistol and then replied, "no you're right, I have a lot on my mind, look, Ryan just get in the car let's get out of here." Ryan looked, as a crowd of people started to assemble, some of them began pointing at Harry believing he was loco. Ryan quickly climbed into the Cadillac. Harry started up the car and pulled off in a rush.

Ryan gazed out of the window at the crowd of people as Harry pressed down on the gas pedal the sun beat down hard, perspiration began to leak from Harry's forehead, they then entered the ethnic dark community. Ryan shook his head gazing out of the car window at all that was going on. "My God Harry this place is intoxicating with low life's, look at the gang bangers, the slobs and gutter punks, look at them." Harry then spoke in a confident voice, "Ryan let us both snap out of our negative vibes we got to visit the Chief, let's stay focused or he will destroy us." Harry drove closer and closer to Chief Mellor's office.

Inspector Francis and Sergeant Canter arrived in Washington D.C. by private jet, they were greeted by two FBI agents both well-dressed. The pickup was arranged a couple of days before. The Inspector introduced himself and the Sergeant. "Hi, my name is Inspector Francis and this man beside me is Sergeant Canter."

one of the FBI agents stepped forward, he had gleaming teeth and tender looks he then spoke in a warm confident voice, " Hi Inspector Francis, we have been instructed to escort you and your Sergeant to our office for a debriefing, the agents then produced their identification cards and then carried on with their introduction. "My name is agent Smith, and this is agent Daniels." Inspector Francis then said, "yes I see, before we go, I would like to point out we are here to find the young man that was kidnapped from my patch in Paris and brought here. it makes my blood boil to think that poor innocent boy is being held captive by two homicidal maniacs and two CIA agents were involved. "

Agent Smith was dedicated to the job clean-shaven his suit was tailored to perfection, he reached into his pocket and produced a pair of designer shades, he put them on then spoke in an authoritative voice, " I will ignore your last comment Sir, in our country we have a strict code of practice, innocent until proven guilty. Do not say another word on this matter, you are on American soil, you must follow our protocol, do I make myself clear?"

Inspector Francis gritted his teeth and just nodded. The agent then said, "okay we understand each other, this way." Inspector Francis and Sergeant Canter followed the two FBI agents to their car, Agent Smith opened the car door, and everyone got in. Agent Smith smiled and then turned to Inspector Francis and said, " sorry about before, I love this job and sometimes get carried away, maybe you are right we have done a lot of digging, Daisy and Harry were once an item we will be putting a tail on him. I believe eventually he will lead us to the kidnapped boy. I believe the two agents Harry and Ryan shall be reporting to Chief Mellor, we have not informed him of our suspicions because of his volatile nature, he may slip up. We will pay him a visit later after Harry and Ryan have been to see him, does all that I have said put your mind at ease?" Inspector Francis nodded and then replied, "yes."

Harry parked his Cadillac in the car park after passing through security his mind whispered, "stay cool stay calm". Ryan turned to Harry and then said, "okay this is it are you nervous?" Harry replied, "no not at all." Ryan then said, "are you sure?" Harry replied, "I just said so didn't I?" Just let me do the talking okay?" Ryan replied, "Harry my lips are sealed." Harry laughed and then said, "good, let's get it over with."

Harry lead the way from the car and into the headquarters, inside as they pass through the reception Harry opened a security door with a pass, they walked through an office, they both received cold looks, after all, their mission was surrounded by controversy. Harry put on a false smile as Ryan hung his head in shame.

They soon arrived at Chief Mellor's office. Harry knocked twice on the door and then a loud voice, said, "Come in." Harry looked to Ryan and grinned. Ryan took a deep breath and then they both entered the room.

Chief Mellor sat in front of his desk; he was a very tall large man with an overwhelming presence. he looked them both up and down he then said, "right take a seat." Harry sat down still grinning. Chief Mellor then spoke in an angry voice, "why are you grinning you son of a bitch? where are your reports?"

Harry reached in his pocket then he produced two pieces of paper from within his pocket, he then replied, "here you are two reports." He placed them on the table, the Chief picked them up and then shook his head he then spoke in a firm voice, " What are you playing at? these reports haven't been filled in properly, you two ain't moving until the reports are filled in properly."

Harry shook his head in disbelief he then spoke in a deep voice, "this is bullshit." Chief Mellor gazed at Harry in disbelief he then spoke with anger in his voice, "do as you are told, or you are both fired is that understood?" Harry replied, "so what? fire us." The chief became even more angry he gritted his teeth then said, "don't push me, Harry."

Ryan began to panic, he couldn't afford to lose his job, he was truly debt-ridden. He tried desperately to calm the situation down. he then spoke, " Chief, Harry didn't mean what he just said, he has been beating himself up, somehow he feels responsible for the poor innocent kid being kidnapped, he just wants to be on the streets looking for the kid, filling in more reports in Harry's eyes is wasting valuable time. We could visit a couple of informers we might even get a lead on where the kid is being kept."

the Chief closed his eyes and imagined some good coming out of this mess, he then opened them and said, "alright you two got five days to find the kid or you're fired how does that sound?" Harry replied, "that to me sounds patronising." Ryan began to panic once more, he then turned to Harry and said, "We got to find that kid or I will lose everything." Ryan became hysterical and spoke in an angry voice, "fuck you, Harry just because you got nothing to lose."

Harry sat grinning again his mind whispered stay calm, stay calm he then said, "Chief, leave Ryan just sack me." The Chief smiled and said, "Alright I will sack you, and Ryan, I will demote you to a less demanding role."

Harry without warning suddenly stood up and walked towards the door in a trance-like state. Ryan looked to the Chief, his lips were crying out for mercy, the Chief laughed out loud and then mumbled: "I finally got rid of you two rejects."

Ryan stood up and walked towards Harry and then totally out of character he shouted back "Mellor, you ain't nothing but a Muppet." Chief Mellor is enjoying himself so much he smiled and then said, "Which one, the Kermit the frog?" Ryan replied, "No Miss Piggy." Chief Mellor laughed out loud then said, "oh fair enough, you pair of dimwits have five days to deliver and close the door on your way out."

Harry turned around to Chief Mellor and spoke with a bewildering look, "how does it feel to be sitting behind a desk with so much power?" The Chief replied, "Harry, it sure feels good."

Harry shrugged his shoulders and then said, "well that's all right then." Harry smiled at the Chief once more, his mind whispered, "stay calm." Harry walked out of the office first followed by his partner in crime. The door, it needed closing. Ryan grabbed hold of the handle, Harry turned to Ryan shaking his head he then spoke in a quiet voice, "no, just leave it, Chief Mellor doesn't bite."

The Chief smiled, aware of the situation he smiled once more and then said, "oh just leave the door open I need a bit of fresh air." Harry said to Ryan, "You alright?" Ryan replied, "no what the fuck Harry? Mad Mellor has been waiting to sack us for years, we got five days to find that kid."

They walked through the office again, funny looks and snide remarks echoed all around, Harry suddenly lost his cool for a brief second and said, " what the fuck are you all looking at?" Complete silence and then the exit door. Harry and Ryan made their way towards the Cadillac, a car passes them and then parks near the front entrance to the station, four men get out of the car. Ryan looked over to the car he then turned to Harry and said, "look Harry it's those guys from Paris that interrogated us." Harry turned slowly and looked towards the four men, Inspector Francis and Sergeant Canter, "the other two guys are FBI, Harry they're going to see Chief Mellor, that means they are on to us."

Harry scratched his head then spoke in a calm voice, "yes it does we have to find Daisy and Peter quick." Ryan then spoke in a cold, calm voice, "Harry you got the shotguns in the boot?" Harry replied, "yes I got the weapons."

Harry got into his Cadillac closely followed by Ryan. Harry took hold of the wheel he then pressed his foot down on the gas pedal. Inspector Francis looked towards the Cadillac pulling away from the office he then said, "did you see who was in that Cadillac Sergeant?" the Sergeant replied, "yes, I did the two rough CIA agents, Harry and Ryan." They then were escorted by the FBI agents to see Chief Mellor.

The radiant glory of the midsummer's day suddenly began to take effect on Harry, he began to sweat furiously this made him angry he then spoke in a loud voice, "What the hell, I need a drink; a nice cold beer. Fancy a drink or two at Len Circ's Irish bar?" Ryan replied, "Len circs Irish bar what a dive it's full of clowns." Harry laughed and then said, "yes, I know the score Ryan he makes all the money and treats the staff like slaves, long hours, low pay the guy's a crook. Ryan, do you remember that conversation I had with him? He informed me he packed in spud picking and entered the circus, performing a knife-throwing act and never looked back. He saved all of his money he had made and brought Len Circ's lowlife bar."

Ryan laughed and said, "You're right about one thing, he still loves stabbing people in the back, okay let's go." Harry made a right turn down a side road a sharp left he then parked up. Ryan turned to Harry and said, "what you reckon about the kid?" Harry looked at Ryan with a fixed expression and then replied, "Look, I need a beer to cool and chill out, we will look for the kid later. I am buying you a beer."

Ryan then said, "Okay Harry if you say so Harry replied, "I do say so now let's go." Harry then got out of the Cadillac and walked towards the bar with Ryan closely following. They entered the bar; it was exactly how Harry described it full of lowlifes. Harry walked up to the bar, he then turned to Ryan and smiled he then said, "what's your poison pal?" Ryan replied, "oh I will have a nice cold beer." Harry laughed and then said, "good, that's what I'm having."

They both sat down on bar stools. Harry then looked around for Pat and then she appeared. Harry took a deep breath then said, "Look Ryan it's my favourite bar lady, Pat the petal." She smiled as she enjoyed the attention, she then spoke in a soft voice, "Hi you guys what can I do for you?"

Harry smiled, she captivated his eye he then replied, "well I can think of a few things." Pat laughed then said, "I bet you can." Harry gazed at her licking her lips, her tender looks, her long legs and shapely figure, in Harry's eyes she was a goddess.

Harry smiled catching his breath and then spoke with confidence, "I just don't know where to start." Pat laughed and said, "I know, two glasses of our best ice-cold beer is that right?" Harry replied, "did you know Pat, you're my type of lady? all front and telepathic." Pat smiled and said, "I am certainly all front but telepathic, you always order two glasses of ice-cold beer, don't you?" Harry replied, "you're right Pat, perhaps I am a bit on the predictable side."

Pat turned towards the pump and slowly poured two glasses of ice-cold beer, she returned to Harry with the beer. Harry could not take his eyes off the prey; she was wearing a low-cut top and tight denim hot pants. Harry was once more in love, he gazed into her ice-blue eyes as she placed the beers onto the bar.

Ryan looked at Harry shaking his head in disbelief. Harry never noticed, he only had eyes for Pat, he then said, "okay Pat what am I thinking?" Pat replied, "knowing you Harry, it's bound to be sheer lust." Harry took a sip of his ice-cold beer then said, "yeah, it's your sexy outfit, you are my dream babe. Maybe I could take you out sometime is that okay with you?" Pat shook her head and replied, "well actually I met a guy last week." Harry shook his head then said, "why am I always too late?" Pat smiled and replied, "I guess that's life, anyway Harry have you read Len Circ's golden rules?"

Harry gazed over at a poster next to Ryan he then spoke in a heightened voice, "okay Ryan read them out loud and clear." Ryan smiled and then began to read them out. The first, 'Handle the glass with care as Health and safety is always fair. Number two 'Come into work unless you're at death's door or you will die poor. Number three, 'Be grateful for your role, operate like a machine with no soul.' Number four, 'The boss is always right even when he has lost his sight. Number five, You're a link in a chain gang, the weakest link will always sink. Number six, only smile and speak when spoken to. Number seven, Mistakes cannot be made, remember the wrath you will not evade. Number eight, Never think it's unfair, stressed out in pain with little to gain get used to it frankly we just don't care, number. Nine, bonus, I do not pay just work and never play. Number ten, 'Len Circ is here to make money, greed is my feed, complaints I will never read.'"

Harry shook his head in disbelief he then said, "okay Pat one more thing do you still do food here? I could murder a burger with iceberg lettuce on it." Pat shook her head and then replied, "sorry Harry we had a bit of a mutiny, the chef left yesterday and took a new barmaid with him. I guess this place is sinking like the Titanic."

All of a sudden Len Circ appeared he had been listening in on the conversation, there was perspiration leaking from his forehead, he was a giant, bald imposing man. He looked into Harry's eyes and laughed, he then spoke in a deep voice, "never mind Harry, there are plenty more fish in the sea." Harry shook his head, his mind whispered, "The nerve of this guy." He then spoke in an angry, heightened voice, " it was a burger I was after not a fish, why don't you pay your staff the going rate? you treat them like crap, overworked underpaid, no wonder they are all leaving, you greedy golden ruled bastard."

Len smiled and replied, "hey what you going on about? They're all smiling ain't they?" Harry replied, "It's that loaded shotgun behind the bar, that's what keeps them smiling, they're all hoping one day you might use it on yourself." Len shook his head and said, "okay Harry I get the picture, enjoy your beer, have a nice day."

Len moved away from Harry before he got really angry. Harry paid and said, "keep the change." Ryan laughed out loud and the said, "first we had Daisy now we got Pat the Petal, Harry you got a Flower fetish." Harry turned to Ryan and said, "shut it, Ryan, you ain't even funny, okay? Ryan let's take a look around Len Circ's bar and see if we recognise any of the clowns, look over there, Benoski the ex-bellboy, he belonged to a secret society of bellboys, they called themselves the Bellends." Ryan laughed and said, "are you sure? all the gossip in Len Circ's Bar is alleged, but that guy Beno, he looks more like Quasimodo."

Harry sipped his beer then spoke in a heightened voice, "I sense a French theme, who's that sitting next to him, Esmeralda?" Ryan shook his head and said, "Len Circ informed me his nickname is Mr Nutjob, he is Benoski's horrid henchman, he loves his beer and spirits as does Benoski. They sit there all day drinking." Harry shook his head and spoke once more in a heightened voice, "Hey, I recognise the square head and sickly smile you're right Ryan, that is Nutjob, the informer, he would sell his soul to the highest bidder. I reckon it was him who put the finger on Beno and his secret society. They robbed the guests all over the city, his mates all went down except for him yet still they are best buddies. This place is full of crazy characters."

Ryan then said, "are they Russian?" Harry replied, "No they ain't in any hurry to go anywhere, a couple of Soviet blockheads." They then both began to laugh.

In the corner of the bar attached to the wall was a large television screen, on it was Blondie, the song playing was 'Union City Blues'. Harry smiled and said, "my God this brings back memories." He turned to Ryan with a grin of content he then spoke slowly, "Did I ever tell you about the time I met Blondie in the flesh?" Ryan replied, "yeah I am sure you did." Harry then said, " oh, anyway I met her in Washington D.C., I had a conversation with her, I still remember it was on a Sunday, she had the face of an angel so beautiful and petit, do you know what I mean?" Ryan replied, "yeah Harry I get the picture." Harry smiled and then said, "picture this, I wish I could have run away with her there and then to the island of lost souls, I told her I was really touched by her presence here, she was so atomic."

Ryan laughed and then pretended to yawn. Harry suddenly began to shake, he shook his head panic fears fluttered his mind, he looked to Ryan and spoke, anxiety twisted his face, "did you know once you get past forty it's all downhill from there on, the anti-wrinkle cream and hair dye years. I suppose it comes to us all eventually. I noticed Ryan you've been getting a few grey hairs." Ryan shook his head and said, "no I ain't going grey," Harry laughed and said, "I know I am only joking."

Len suddenly reappeared, he looked at Harry with a fixed expression and then spoke, his bald head was gleaming in the light as he began to speak in a voice of concern. "Harry, look over there it's that punk that got drunk and killed that little girl, I haven't seen him around here for years."

Harry remembered the parents of the little girl, he had visions of their tormented faces, their anguish has left a scar in his mind. He turned to Ryan and said, "do you remember him" Ryan replied, "yeah, he killed that little girl in a hit and run, and his mate took the rap." Harry then turned to Len and said, "okay then two Jack Daniel's on the house." Len said, "okay Harry coming up." Len prepared two Jack Daniel's on the rocks in a matter of minutes, he handed the drinks to Harry with a look of confusion."

Ryan looked to Harry and said, "My God Harry, look at that slimeball." Harry picked up his Jack Daniel's, in the blink of an eye, it was gone. Harry then spoke in an angry voice, "Hit and run, I reckon I ought to do that same to him. Harry felt a red mist descending, he gazed over at the punk who was playing pool, he was tall with shoulder-length dark hair, he wore a black T-shirt and jeans.

Suddenly Harry's anger rose until it erupted like a volcano. "God damn you!" he cried out. he quickly moved towards the punk playing pool, the punk turned to face Harry, he then gazed into Harry's eyes with contempt. His body a mass of artwork, he looked extremely haggard, complete with a rebellious barbaric complexion.

He grinned at Harry with his pool cue raised high above his head. Harry moved closer and closer. The punk suddenly remembered Harry, he smiled then spoke, "Hey I remember, ain't you that corrupt agent?" Harry shook his head in disbelief he then replied, "No you got me mixed up with someone else." Harry looked up at the raised pool cue and said, "Did you know that cue is an offensive weapon just like that car you used to kill that little girl? you sick son of a bitch."

The punk began frowning in confusion, he then opened his mouth and said, "Look, man, that was a long time ago, forgive and forget." Harry shook his head trying his best to remain calm, he then said, "It was five years ago, how old was she eight years of age five and eight what is that punk?"

The punk replied, "Err oh that's thirteen." Harry then said, "that's unlucky what day is it punk?" The punk replied once more, "Err reckon it's Friday isn't it?" Harry replied, "Okay punk it's Friday the thirteenth your luck just ran out punk, Harry pulled out his pistol and said, "Say hello to my little friend." the punk automatically said, "Scarface." Harry grinned and said, " who are you calling Scarface ?" The punk shook his head and replied, "No I mean Al Pacino said that in the movie."

Harry gritted his teeth and then spoke in a raised voice, "This ain't no movie, this is real life, drop the cue or I will drop you." Harry moved forward before the punk could react, he punched him in the face, as he fell Harry pistol-whipped the punk across his leg, he fell to the ground knocked out cold.

The punk's friends moved swiftly making a sharp exit out of the bar. Everyone in the bar looked to Harry they all reflected a shade of terror. Harry triumphantly re-holstered his pistol with a comforting sense of fulfilment. Harry shouted out loud so everyone could hear his words, "Good, he won't be driving for a while, sweet justice, the punk got what was coming to him, anyone disagree? if so let me know."

Ryan recognised a face from the past hiding in the corner of the bar Ryan shouted, "Look Harry there's what's his face?" Harry looked to the corner of the room and replied, "you're right it's one of pistol-whipped Peter's mates, Grimbo." "That's right Harry, it's Grimbo Jones, part-time crack dealer, look he's seen us watch him try to disappear."

Grimbo stood up and walked towards the exit. Ryan walked towards him all of a sudden, he changed his direction and headed for the toilets. Harry followed him into the toilet he then pushed open a toilet door, hiding behind it was Grimbo. Harry gritted his teeth and began to speak in a loud, dominant voice, "Hey punk you still need a leak I know who you are, Grimbo Jones, the failed crack dealer."

Grimbo was all skin and bone, several years of taking drugs had taken its toll on his body and craggy face. He looked to Harry with a fixed expression and said, "Hey I know you you're dirty Harry, but you ain't as good looking as Clint Eastwood."

Harry lost his cool and without warning punched Grimbo in the stomach. Grimbo cried out in agony, Harry looked into Grimbo's eyes and then spoke in a firm voice, "Look I am going to ask you a few questions, any backchat and you will get another punch understood?" Grimbo replied, "Look I am sorry Harry what do you want to know?" Harry replied, "That's better, we have an understanding. Your old mate, pistol-whipped Peter, where can I find him?" Grimbo replied, "Look, Harry, me and Peter fell out he's the jealous type, he reckoned I was after his bitch. We ended up fighting and he stuck a blade in my chest."

Grimbo lifted his shirt slowly to reveal a two-inch scar he then said, " because we were once close friends is the only reason he let me live, but he told me if he ever laid eyes on me again he would cut me up into little pieces. Since that day I have given him a wide birth."

Harry gazed down at the scar he then smiled a voice in his head said, " stay cool he then spoke in a quiet voice, " that guy's an animal, when I catch him I am going to have him put down, get my drift?" Grimbo replied as he lowered his shirt, "Yeah Harry I am sorry to waste your time." Harry then said, "okay get out of here after all this excitement it's me that needs a leak."

Ryan entered the toilets and spoke out in a concerned voice, "Harry are you okay in there?" Harry replied, "yeah I am alright just taking a leak." Ryan then said, "what did Grimbo tell you?" Harry washed his hands and then turned to Ryan and replied, " Grimbo is avoiding Peter because Peter informed him if he ever lays eyes on him again he will carve him up, and yes I believe him I think it's in our interest to get out of here."

Harry and Ryan walked towards the exit, there standing before them was larger than life Len Circ. he then said, "Harry I agree, justice has been served, I will get some men to get rid of the body okay?" Harry replied, "Good, looks like the punk's luck just ran out."

Harry and Ryan laughed together as they walked out of Len Circ's bar, they walked over to the Cadillac, Ryan turned to Harry as the radiant sun beat down on them, he then said, "okay where do we start looking for Daisy and Peter?" Harry replied, "alright Ryan, let me ask you a question if you had the kid what would you be doing now?" Ryan replied, "oh that's simple I would be using the kid to make as much money as possible." Harry smiled and then said, "that's what I was thinking, I reckon we visit some betting shops, my friend." Ryan agreed and they both got into the car and drove off.

Back in the warehouse, Boris stood up and removed his T-shirt to reveal a white gold Saint Christopher necklace, his body odour was revolting, he needed a wash. he turned to Daisy and said, "Hey Daisy, is there anywhere I can have a quick wash?" Daisy pointed the far corner of the warehouse, an old sink complete with running water. Boris spoke in a deep voice, " is that it man? It's hardly the Hilton." Peter listened to the door from outside the door where David was being held captive. All of a sudden, he heard David coughing from the locked room. Peter unlocked the door and said, "what's the matter kid?" David replied, "oh it's the damp room, it's making me cough." Peter laughed, then began sniff, he then spoke in a quiet voice, "the rancid smell, my God kid you're right, it stinks. come here let's get you out of there."

Peter took hold of David's arm, again David coughed. Daisy watched in disbelief as Peter escorted David from the damp room. Daisy then spoke in a loud voice, "what's going on?" Peter replied, "Look, Daisy, that room is rancid, the kid has been coughing." "So what?" "I thought we were looking after the kid's best interests." Daisy suddenly began to see thousands of dollar bills before her eyes. Daisy then spoke in a soft voice, "My God Peter you're right, ignore me, sweet child, sometimes I just don't think." Peter agreed and then said, "don't worry the kid ain't stupid he won't try to escape. Here kid, have a bottle of water, I reckon you must need a drink."

Peter passed David a bottle of water. "It's a bit warm kid, but it's better than nothing." All of a sudden, a loud knock at the door. Peter raced towards the door and opened it with great haste. stood before him was Macko with a copy of the racing results. "Macko, have you checked the results?" "No, I thought I'd leave the honour to you."

Peter walked over to the table and sat down, all four gathered around the table. Peter began to match the winning horses with a confident smile he then said, "yes we got the first one." Daisy looked to Peter in amazement, "yes we got the second, third and fourth." Peter suddenly grew hysterical he roared with laughter, "my God! the kid did it, we got all seven horses."

Daisy rubbed David's head she then shouted, " my God David you're a star." They all began to celebrate jumping up and down and hugging each other. Macko turned to Peter with a look of confusion on his face he then said, "how much have we won?" Peter replied, "oh I reckon over eighty thousand dollars." Boris looked to Peter with a face of concern he then spoke in a deep voice, "look man it's alright winning it, but collecting it, but getting it back here safe and sound is a completely different matter."

Macko gritted his teeth and said, "Boris is right, I once robbed two men fresh from the betting shop, they had two thousand-dollar bills, word spreads around fast the local gang bangers will be out in force, this is a rough neighbourhood." Macko opened up his holdall and produced two semi-automatic weapons he then said, "me and Boris will collect the money, I need you to watch my back understood?" Boris replied, "don't worry man, no one is going to mess with us."

Macko handed Boris the weapon, he then placed it inside his jeans and then pulled his Bob Marley T-shirt over it. Peter handed Macko the betting slip, he could not believe his luck, eighty thousand dollars a voice in his head now whispered, "Something is going to go wrong." His whole life had revolved around bad luck. the day he met Daisy things dived to a new low, on his first date he was robbed and beaten to an inch of his life. He was born on the thirteenth of January, and yes it was a Friday. since that day he bore the scars of it.

Peter was suddenly gripped by a hot flush panic, he had a macabre vision, anxiety twisting his face. Daisy looked to Peter, confused "what's wrong Honey?" Peter replied, "oh I had a vision of everything going wrong as usual." Daisy then said, "poor Peter, why are you always having negative visions?" Peter replied, "oh I am sorry Daisy I just can't believe the kid weaved his magic and eighty thousand dollars appeared, I reckon it's a miracle."

Macko became inpatient and then spoke in a deep voice, "alright, me and Boris are now leaving to collect the money and if anyone gets in our way, I will waste them." Peter smiled and said, "Macko do what you have to do." Macko turned to Boris with a look of determination, he then said, "let us be on our way."

Macko and Boris then left to collect the money. Daisy turned to Peter and then spoke in a low voice, "sugar you're sweet but you do pathetically worry over nothing, those guys are born killers nothing is going to get in their way, isn't that why we picked them out?" Peter replied, "Yeah Daisy I got to start thinking more positively."

Peter smiled and then turned to David and spoke in a low voice, "kid how did you pull that off? you're a priceless treasure, I can't wait until lottery day. Daisy, we are going to be rich, do you agree?" Daisy replied, "I know but what about the Chuckle Brothers?" Peter replied, "what about them? now you are being negative, we got two badass killers to sort them out." Daisy then said, "Yeah we could let them do all the gunplay and sneak off with the money what you reckon?" Peter replied, "My, Daisy self-preservation that's a great idea." Daisy then said, "honey if it wasn't, my lips would be sealed."

Daisy embraced Peter; their lips met as they kissed each other. David knew it was his opportunity to escape, he stood up and began to walk past them towards the exit. all of a sudden, a loud voice rang in David's ears, David turned around, he stood rooted with fear, Daisy then spoke in a loud voice, "David darling, I got a semi-automatic pistol pointing at you are you going somewhere?" David replied, "well I wanted a quick wash in the sink, I was going to ask your permission but you two were sort of preoccupied." Daisy then said, "that's correct kid we were kissing, anyway how is your cough?" "oh, it seems to be a bit better." "good, that's nice to know, go ahead have a wash but just remember if you try to escape, I will have to shoot you, okay?"

Peter disagreed and said, "over my dead body, you can't shoot the kid." Daisy shook her head in disbelief, she then said, "carry on kid have a wash." David turned and carried on with his journey towards the sink. Daisy turned to Peter and expressed her annoyance she then spoke in a low voice, "would you like keeping your voice down, I was only trying to frighten the kid, do you honestly think I would shoot the kid?"

Daisy pushed Peter and they both began to laugh out loud. David turned on the tap and washed his face in the cold water, he used paper towels to dry his face, he then returned to the table and sat down. Peter then said, "good kid I got some more candy bars, here do you want them?" David nodded his head, Peter then handed him the candy bars. Daisy gazed into Peter's eyes and said, "My God! you're good with children, we ought to have some of our own one day, what you reckon?" Peter replied, "I would make a good sugar Daddy, the poor kids would live off candy bars when we going to get some real food?" Daisy replied, "as soon as the guys get back with the cash, we shall have a party, lots of food and drink, you promised David a burger and fries I wonder how they are getting on?"

Macko and Boris walked towards the bookmakers as the sun beat down. Macko knew his only chance of returning with the money in one piece was Boris watching his back. Macko felt a need to remind Boris of the fact. Macko looked to Boris and spoke with a voice of authority. "remember you are my back up if anyone comes up behind me shoot them dead understood?" Boris replied, "loud and clear man, no one is going to take our money off us, I will keep a close eye on the street.

Boris looked all around; he saw a gang of drug dealers going about their business. in the distance, the noise of the traffic which began to ring in his ears, this was a vile place where life had little meaning. they carried on walking, the sun showed no mercy, there was a cool breeze. all of a sudden, the sound of Salsa music echoed all around the streets, they soon arrived at the betting shop. inside and outside the shop the news that someone had won on a seven-horse accumulator had spread fast, the manager had employed two armed guards just in case of any trouble. they stood waiting, and then his eyes perked with curiosity as the two tall mysterious strangers entered the shop.

the two guards reflected shades of terror as they gazed at Macko. The manager recognised him and said, "that's him the man who put on the bet." Macko did not like all of the attention he approached the manager and spoke with a calm voice, "look let's keep this low key, all I want is the money, here you are the copy of the betting slip."

Macko reached inside his pocket and produced it, he then handed it to the manager. The manager then said, "I believe your poor father picked out these horses on his death bed, the odds on these horses all finishing first are remote." Macko tried to remain calm he then spoke in a calm voice, "look I just want the money, my poor father is dead now so don't worry, it won't be happening again alright do you understand?" The manager replied, "no fuss, you just want to pay out well come with me into my office and I will settle your winnings."

Macko followed the manager into his office the manager then said, "right sir take a seat." Macko replied, "no I just want the money as quickly as possible." the manager then said, "yes well would you except a cheque made payable to your good self?" Macko began to shake with impatience he gritted his teeth, sweating furiously and then his anger erupted like a volcano he shouted, "look just give me the cash now!"

the manager began to blink and frown, his heart was pounding as he gazed at Macko, his face filled with anger. the manager then said, "Sir will you not have a drink and except my hospitality? it's over eighty thousand dollars, the streets out there show you no mercy, maybe our company could invest your winnings for you." Macko replied, "no thank you just give me my money."

The manager knew he was wasting his time and then said, "I have it here in the safe it will take me a few minutes to count it out in front of you is that okay?" Macko replied, "no need, I trust you."

The manager then said, "my, Sir you are in a hurry, I won't keep you waiting any longer, I will put the money straight into this holdall. You know that once the money leaves the premises it is no longer insured? what I am really trying to say is watch your back, you may be a target word travels fast in this neighbourhood."

Macko then said, "do not concern yourself no one is going to take the money off me." The manager finished off putting the dollars into the holdall he then said, "right Sir would you like to make some more money? my brother is a reporter, your story about your poor departed father picking out these horses on his death bed would make a good story, my brother would pay you good money for such a story."

Macko shook his head and then and said, " no need, I lied about the story now just give me the money." The manager, a sharp dressed man of medium and build with very pale skin, he looked to Macko with a sense of compulsion, he then said, "alright just take the money, you won it fair and square, take the money."

Macko picked up the holdall filled with dollars, the manager opened the door to his office and Macko walked out, he handed the bag to Boris with an angry glare he spoke with words of steel "Don't you dare lose it."

Macko looked all around everyone on the street looked to the holdall containing the dollars. Macko and Boris began to sweat but they were professional killers, they did not know the concept of fear. the security guards escorted Macko and Boris onto the streets away from the betting shop Boris looked to Macko and said, "look, man at all of the faces, they all know we have the money let's get the hell out of here quickly as possible."

Macko and Boris took long strides as they rushed from the betting office, suddenly it was Macko's worst nightmare, Chiquita and Juan and two of their men, they were life's lowest of the lows, they pulled alongside Macko and Boris driving slowly in a red open convertible. they were Mexicans.

nothing moved unless they said so. murder and crime were a way of life to them they all looked alike, dark hair and very tanned skin. Macko looked, he saw a familiar face, it was Chiquita. a smile, a laugh he then began to speak. "Macko, my old friend I've been watching to see who collected the big win, I didn't expect you to come out with the bag of money, you must be collecting it for someone."

Macko replied, "yes, I get ten per cent to deliver it, that's good is it not? Chiquita looked to Juan with a smile on his face and said, "what do you think Juan is that a good offer?" Juan laughed, Chiquita then turned his attention to Macko, he then said, " hey Macko where is your bag of tricks? you look naked without your bag of tricks, I know, you give me the money and I give you ten per cent, what do you reckon? I am being fair am I not?"

a voice in Macko's mind whispered, "kill or be killed." with the blink of an eye Macko pulled out his pistol and started to fire at the Mexicans, he emptied the whole magazine into the convertible, all four died instantly.

Macko looked at the blood-stained; bullet-ridden convertible with death cold eyes. he then scanned all around the streets stood still in silence, and then the noise of shouts and sirens. Macko turned to Boris with a voice of concern, "we need to get out of here now."

Macko started to run from the crime scene, Boris followed, escaping before the Police arrived. Boris hung on tight to the bag of money, they ran along the unforgiving streets, they then took a sharp left passing several abandoned buildings. in the far distance, they could hear the sound of Police sirens.

Peter stood by the door, he could hear the sounds coming from the street, he stood still in disbelief. as

Macko and Boris ran towards him he opened the door wide, as they all entered the warehouse Peter looked to Macko in a confused state and then spoke with a voice of concern, "what happened? this was hardly low key,"

Macko took a deep breath, the escape had left his heart pounding. he then replied slowly, "word got out, then the Mexicans appeared, they wanted to collect the money I said no to them with my gun."

Peter shook his head and said, "my God! I hate those Mexican bandits." Daisy looked at Boris her mind whispered, "thousands of dollars" she then said, "okay show us the money."

Boris tipped out the contents of the bag onto the table, everyone's eyes lit up at the sight. Macko looked to Peter and said, "I believe you owe me a large chunk of that money, I just killed four Mexicans, I am now a target on the streets, their brothers will come after me."

Peter looked into Macko's eyes and spoke in a calm voice, "look Macko we have been friends for many years, we still need your services, won't you stick around until the end of the week? believe me, your thousands will become millions, you both have seen nothing yet, this kid is going to predict the Lottery numbers and we will collect one hundred million dollars, how cool is that my friend? You could come out of this with twenty-five million dollars."

Macko listened to Peter, his words rang in his ears, an offer he could not refuse, the sort of offer no one could refuse. Macko quickly forgot all of his problems that sort of money could place him in early retirement, he could live like a king. Macko then grinned and spoke in a deep voice, "I like the sound of twenty-five million, will I stick around until the end of the week? my answer has to be yes."

Daisy looked to Boris with a smile and said, "look man, twenty-five million dollars." Peter looked around at everyone's faces he then said, "alright that's settled then everyone gets a twenty-five million share." Peter then looked at Daisy and said, "I reckon the heat's on us now we need to go to plan b, we need to change our appearance and our location."

Daisy opened a large case and began to pull out various wigs and dark sunglasses. Daisy put on a blonde wig and a pair of sunglasses

she then said, "look Peter what you reckon?" Peter replied, "you look like that famous Hollywood actress, what was her name? that's it, Marylin Munroe." Boris shook his head he then spoke in his usually laid-back voice, "No man, Marylin Munroe is dead and so will we be if we don't get something to eat."

Daisy looked at Boris, she knew he was becoming impatient, she then said, "alright I've got on my disguise why don't I slip out and get us some food and drink?" David sat quietly reading an old book he had found in a drawer; it was a very popular book entitled the Bible.

Daisy left the warehouse to purchase some food and drink, no one stood in her way.

Harry sat listening to the Police radio, he turned to Ryan, "this might be what I've been waiting for a homicide, four Mexicans wasted next to where eighty thousand dollars was paid out on a seven-horse accumulator. they reckon the Mexicans attempted to rob the dollars and were shot to pieces what you reckon?" Ryan replied, "well Harry, Peter and Daisy ain't in the Mexican's league, I reckon they have hired some urban killers." Harry agreed. he then started up his car and then hit the gas pedal, Ryan turned to Harry and said, "where we off to then?" Harry replied, "oh, twenty-fifth street, that was where the action is happening."

Inspector Francis and Sergeant Canter were one step ahead, they had arrived with the FBI agents. they began questioning witnesses. Agent Smith then turned to Inspector Francis and said, "two men were collecting winnings from the bookmakers when these bandits tried to rob them and paid for it with their lives. I have spoken to the Manager of the shop he said the bet was placed and paid out over eighty thousand dollars."

Inspector Francis looked to Agent Smith and the spoke in a deep voice, "what was the sum placed on the seven-horse accumulator?" The agent replied, " oh I believe it was three hundred dollars or less what are you thinking ?" the Inspector replied, " I believe this is the work of David, their undoing will be their greed, these two men what of their escape ?"

the agent replied, "I was informed they escaped on foot." Inspector Francis smiled and said, "good, then we shall find them eventually in these surroundings have you a map of the area Agent Smith?" the agent replied, "yes, I believe they ran in that direction, several miles of abandoned buildings. I reckon that is where they will be trying to keep a low profile."

Harry drove towards the crime scene, Ryan looked again and again at a vehicle behind them he then said, "Harry did you know we are being followed?" Harry replied, "yes I know I will lose them later." Harry parked up near the crime scene, he and Ryan climbed out of the car. Harry focused his eyes in disbelief, he then turned to Ryan and said, "my God it's Inspector Francis, he is always one step ahead of us, look Ryan over there, it's those FBI guys."

Ryan then said, "I know Harry you stand by the car I will go and have a word with the Detective." Harry agreed with a nod of his head. Ryan walked over to the Detective, he then got out his identification badge and spoke, "Hi I am a CIA agent, what happened here? this might be connected to a case we are working on."

the Detective gazed at Ryan's identification then spoke, "I see your name is Ryan, my name is John. to cut a long story short, two guys collected eighty thousand dollars from the betting office, these four bandits tried to rob them and one of the two pulled out a gun and emptied the magazine into them. I have just heard from a witness, for twenty dollars he gave me a name, a killer by the name of Macko."

Ryan looked into the Detectives eyes and said, "the name rings a bell." the Detective was tall with eyes as wide as the ocean. Ryan suddenly made a connection but kept the information to himself. Ryan smiled at the Detective and said, " one more thing Detective, did they escape on foot or car?" the Detective replied, " oh I believe they ran off in that direction, in two hours we are going to be sweeping across that area searching all the abandoned buildings. would you like to accompany us?" Ryan laughed and then replied, "well thank you for your kind invitation but me and my buddy have other work to attend to." Ryan shook the Detectives hand and then turned around and walked over to Harry.

Ryan shook his head his mind whispered, "machine gun Macko." Ryan then approached Harry and then said, "oh Harry I thought you said Peter wasn't very intelligent, well guess who he has hired? only machine gun Macko, what you reckon to that?" Harry replied, "Shit he's one mean mother fucker". The guys a born killer. What else did the say?" Ryan replied, "oh Macko killed the four Mexicans then he escaped on foot with some other guy in that direction. The detective said, in two hours they will be sweeping across that area looking for Macko and the rest of them."

Harry looked to Ryan he took a deep breath and then spoke, "are you up for this? Macko is a hard man to kill, I remember reading a report on Macko he's killed dozens, he's taken quite a few bullets on the way. His people reckon bullets simply bounce off him, his trademark is his holdall filled with weapons." Ryan scratched his head then said, "I reckon we have come too far to back down Harry I am up for this, I reckon that eighty thousand dollars belongs to us."

Harry put on a brave face and said, "yeah that's the spirit I have been doing some thinking, I reckon the other guy is bad Boris, you know the Caribbean fella?" "yeah wasn't he on good terms with Daisy?" Harry replied, "yeah that's the one. Listen, Ryan, we got two hours before the sweep starts, I got a feeling I might know where they are holed up, the southside, that old warehouse. I reckon they are there."

Inspector Francis looks over at Harry in deep thought, he then turned to Sergeant Canter and said, "Look at them two they are also looking for Daisy and Peter. I believe they were double-crossed and are also looking, very soon all of this will eventually end in a lot of bloodshed."

Harry and Ryan climbed into the Cadillac and pulled off slowly. Harry looked in his rear-view mirror and said, "Right Ryan is that car still on our tail?" Ryan replied, "Yes, it's the same one as before." Harry suddenly made a sharp right, he put his foot on the pedal he then made a sharp left. The tail car followed but Harry knew the area well and soon lost the tail car.

Harry sat tensely he then smiled with a comforting sense of fulfilment. He then spoke in a confident voice,

"Ryan did you see how quickly I lost that tail? it takes years of practice to get that good." Ryan laughed then said, "Harry I can't get over that kid, he turned three hundred dollars into eighty thousand dollars that is amazing! I can't believe she ripped us off, that kid could have made enough money for all of us."

Harry agreed. he then drove along slowly he scanned ahead one particular person caught his eye he then said, "look Ryan that blonde with the bags, look at the walk I recognise that walk, it's Daisy in a blonde wig isn't it?" Ryan replied, "you reckon?" Harry replied, "yeah I just said, so didn't I? look Ryan, she's making her way to that abandoned warehouse, I reckon we take her out before she gets to the warehouse, we could exchange her for the kid. I know Peter loves her, look what he did to that Grimbo character."

Harry put his foot down on the gas pedal, Ryan opened his window and pulled out his semi-automatic pistol, Harry slammed on the brakes as Ryan jumped out of the car, he pointed his pistol at Daisy and then spoke with a voice of authority. "Daisy, you move and I'm going to put a hole in you." Daisy dropped her bags and then turned around slowly, anxiety twisted her face as her eye lids fluttered.

Harry then jumped out of his car, he then opened his boot and produced a pump-action shotgun, he threw it to Ryan. he then gazed at Daisy, he was angry and spoke in a heightened voice, "you double-crossing bitch! stay perfectly still." Harry then said, "I know you would love to turn and run off, wouldn't you? if you do, I will blow your legs off. Ryan go ahead cuff her she ain't going nowhere. I know how much she loves her legs."

Daisy nervously smiled and said, "hey I still remember the days when you liked these pretty legs sugar you remember?" Harry replied, "that was a long time ago, people change, you certainly did from an angel to a demon."

Daisy changed her voice, with a sense of compulsion she spoke in a loud voice, "Harry you make me sick, if I am a demon then you are the Devil! Dirty Harry, the most corrupt cop of all time. does your partner know about all of the corruption you got up to in the early days?"

Harry felt a red mist descending, he then lost control he then spoke in a loud voice, "hurry up Ryan cuff her and gag her, I am sick and tired of listening to her lies." Daisy laughed and then said, "but Harry you know they are not lies." Ryan put down his shotgun back into the boot and then cuffed her pulling her hands tight behind her back.

Daisy became more abusive and then said, "go easy, my God! Oh, by the way, did Harry ever tell you he had a thing for your Cindy doll?" Harry erupted like a volcano, he stepped forward unleashing a punch that hit her in the nose, she fell back. Daisy felt dazed as blood poured from her nose which was now broken. Harry then spoke in a loud voice, "I told you to keep your mouth shut."

Ryan looked to Harry in confusion he then said, "what did she mean you had a thing for her?" Harry shook his head and replied, "don't you understand what she is trying to do divide and conquer? she is trying to get us to fight each other." Daisy became angry and then hysterical she then shouted, "God I hate you look at my nose it's broken! look at what you have done."

Harry took a deep breath then replied, "look, Daisy, keep it down or next it will be your front teeth." Daisy knew he wasn't joking and adopted a decent approach, she smiled and then she suddenly began to choke on the blood now pouring from her nose. Ryan then shouted, "shit Harry couldn't you have punched her elsewhere?"

Ryan reached into his pocket and produced some tissues, he then began to stem the flow of blood Harry then spoke in a dominant voice, "Ryan get her into the car don't matter about the blood I will clean it up later." Ryan pushed Daisy into the back seat, Daisy laughed out loud as Harry sat down in the driving seat. Ryan then said, "okay Daisy how are we going to play this?" Daisy replied, "I reckon you want to exchange me for the kid, well you can have him I have made my money who cares?"

Harry turned to Daisy and said, "no Daisy I think not, the way I intend to play." Harry looked into Daisy's eyes and then carried on talking, "the fact is, I don't like being double-crossed there was enough money for everyone, you just got greedy. I intend on having all the money your stupid bitch!" Daisy put on a false smile and said, " come on Harry, you got to leave us some of the money, we got Macko and Boris with us if you don't pay them they will kill you both you got a death wish ?" Harry replied, "who cares? listen to me I want all the money."

Daisy suddenly lost her cool and then spoke in a loud voice, "shit Harry you're so cold-hearted what about your partner? Ryan does he not have a say on his death." Harry laughed then replied, "Ryan trusts me, you don't have any say in this matter, just do as your told. now show us where the money is"?

Daisy replied, "it's the next warehouse, why couldn't you have turned up five minutes later?" Harry smiled and then replied, "I believe it was fate no one double-crosses me and lives to tell the tale if you know what I mean?" Daisy looked to Harry with a face filled with fear she replied, "what Harry you're going to shoot me?" Harry laughed then replied, "yeah right between the eyes." Daisy then said, "look Harry let me go, I will have a chat with the guys and see if we can all come to some arrangement without any bloodshed, what do you think?"

Harry replied, "do you think I am stupid? you know that ain't going to happen." Daisy gave Harry a defiant look, her anger erupted like a volcano she then shouted, "you mad bastard! what this means we're all about to die." Harry smiled, enjoying the moment watching Daisy panic, revenge was sweet he thought, he then said, "all except me and my partner, it's about self-preservation." Ryan smiled and then said, "Harry you got a plan then? I require enlightenment."

Harry replied, "well my fellow trooper what we need is some cannon fodder." Harry then turned his attention to Daisy madness engulfed his eyes as he spoke, "right Daisy back to you the entrance into the warehouse is there an exit?" Daisy searched her memory with a look of disbelief on her face she replied, "yeah Harry, right at the back of the building what are you planning?" Harry replied, "right, to business!"

his mind began to fill with excitement. Harry picked up his mobile he then turned to Ryan and said, "right Ryan remember those guys that owe us a favour, Rob and his mate odd job?" Ryan replied, "Harry do you mean Rob and James?" Harry replied, "yeah that's them, our cannon fodder, understand my method?" Ryan replied, "you mean you're going to get them to go through the main entrance whilst we go around the back?" Harry replied, "yeah great minds think alike."

Daisy shook her head in disgust, she then said, "Harry you're so cold-hearted." Harry drew a deep breath, he thought enough is enough, he then spoke in a cool voice, "Ryan gag her." Ryan looked to Harry with a face of confusion as Harry opened the glove compartment, Ryan then said, "what with Harry?" Harry got out an old rag, Daisy became hysterical her face frozen with fear, she then shouted, "no don't do it." Harry laughed out loud and said, "only joking Ryan use the tape."

Harry turned to Daisy and then said, "look lady cooperate or take a bullet you never know maybe you might survive all this." Daisy knew Harry wasn't joking and allowed Ryan to place the tape over her mouth, she then lay down in the back of the car. Harry then contacted Rob on his mobile phone a brief delay and then Rob answered. "Hi Rob, it's your best buddy, Harry are you ready to return that favour you owe me? James was driving along he looked to his partner and said, "who is it, Rob?" Rob replied, "look be quiet, it's Harry. look Harry what is it you want?"

Harry replied, "well my friend that missing kid from France I have found him that's why I have contacted you. why should me and my partner Ryan take all the glory?" James stopped at a set of lights; he was solidly built with a strange looking forehead complete with dull brown eyes. he sat chewing his bottom lip as Harry and Rob talked. He then hung up. James didn't trust Harry he then spoke with a voice of concern, "okay Rob what does he want?" Rob replied as he looked to James and then said, "after the lights have changed get a move on, Harry has found the kid kidnapped from France, he says he doesn't want to take all the glory, he wants us to take some of the credit."

James shook his head then said, "what? that guy's an animal can we trust him?" Rob replied, "look take a left drive to the old warehouse, the kid's being held hostage there, Harry says it was Daisy and Peter that kidnapped him. Harry has Daisy hostage he's gonna do a swap with

Peter, Daisy for the kid. he needs us as back up, I reckon he's just covering every angle, I trust him, he saved my ass once or twice." Rob's memories came flooding back to him, James continued to drive faster and faster.

the weather was overcast as the sun tried to beat a stubborn cloud formation. a few moments passed all of a sudden, Rob became very nervous, he rubbed his eyes, he had an uneasy feeling and became gripped by a hot flush panic. James knew Rob hadn't told him the whole story; he became furious. he lifted his foot off the gas pedal driving at a slow pace he turned to Rob and said, "look what haven't you told me? remember the four dead Mexicans?"

Rob replied, "shit you mean machine gun, Macko?" James replied, "yeah that's why they need back up." James then pulled over to the side just before they reached Harry grinding to a halt he then spoke out loud with fear in his eyes, "Machine gun Macko! are you mad? we are going to get ourselves killed, that ain't my idea of a favour to Harry, it's a god damn army that's what we need if we're going up against machine gun Macko. I ain't going in without more back up."

Rob sat quietly thinking for a brief second he then said, "I reckon you're right, I got a plan, as soon as the shooting begins, I will call for backup, that ought to make you feel better." James scanned all around he then spoke, "it's quiet around here." they were surrounded by derelict buildings the sound of seagulls on the wing echoed from the sky.

James then pulled off slowly gaining confidence, he knew what had to be done. Rob looked up ahead he turned to his partner and said, "look up ahead it's Harry and Ryan." James forced a smile and said, "look, I know Harry is bad, but I reckon Ryan is okay." Rob nodded in agreement. James pulled up behind Harry's car.

back inside the warehouse, Peter became edgy. he turned to his friend, Macko, his mind plagued with fear he then spoke, "Macko what's taking her so long? she's been gone for ages, do you think something has happened to her?" Macko smiled, he knew no fear he then replied, "hey Peter if she isn't back in the next half an hour I myself will go out and find her."

David sat looking at Peter's face, he knew Harry had her, whenever he closed his eyes, he could see events unfolding from within his mind's eye. Harry opened his car door, his mind cried out judgement day! he climbed out of his car and approached Rob who also got out of his car. he stood still as Harry greeted him. "Hi Rob, I have a plan, me and Ryan will go to the back exit and sneak up behind them as you come in from the front." Rob shook his head in disbelief then spoke, "you got to be kidding me! machine gun Macko is in there isn't he?" Harry replied, "yeah, I know remember those stun grenades? I got some in my boot all you and James have to do is create a diversion, just throw a couple of them in. the element of surprise understands?" Rob replied, "ok Harry but me and James ain't going inside the warehouse with machine gun Macko in there, not without an army."

Harry became enraged, he gritted his teeth and spoke, "look here, I've put my neck out for you in the past you owe me this favour." Rob shook his head then spoke, "no Harry me and my partner ain't taking on Macko in any suicidal gunplay." Harry shrugged his shoulders and then said, "oh okay have it your way just throw in the grenades when I send you a message on your mobile, and just drive away." Rob then said, "okay Harry no hard feelings, after this is over you can buy me a beer and we can talk about the good old days."

Harry forced a smile, he reached out and shook Rob's hand he then spoke, "nice one buddy I got the box of grenades." Harry walked over to his car he opened his boot and produced a box, as Rob explained to James about Harry's plan. James smiled and said, "so all he wants us to do is throw a couple of grenades?" Rob replied, "yeah that's what he says, just to create a diversion." "Good, then we can call for backup." "yeah that's what we are going to do but Harry doesn't need to know."

Harry handed the box to Rob. Harry looked into Rob's eyes and said, "remember when I send the message." Rob nodded his head and then spoke, "okay Harry, me and James have it all in hand.

Harry opened his car door and then got in, he then drove to the back of the warehouse and then parked up. Ryan got out of the car he then pulled Daisy out, she struggled but to no avail as Ryan had a tight grip of her arms. Harry strolled over to Daisy and said, "I am going to remove the tape are you going to make me regret this decision yes or no? just shake your head."

Daisy shook her head as Harry removed the tape slowly Daisy shook her head, anxiety twisted her face, she licked her lips, her heart was pounding. Harry looked at Daisy with a fixed expression Daisy frowned in confusion, she was gripped by a hot flush she then said with an expression of complete horror, "Harry I reckon we're all about to die."

Harry could sense her fear he then spoke in a calm voice, "okay Daisy tell me what else I can do, I want the kid do you understand?" Daisy replied, "okay Harry you win, I have a good idea, a plan where no one gets killed." Harry then said, "my God! Daisy, you should have told me this earlier."

Daisy put a brave face on and then spoke, "I couldn't you put tape across my mouth remember?" Harry replied, "yeah that was stupid of me okay tell me your plan." Daisy replied, "how about I call Peter with your mobile, explain my situation tell him not to inform the others? I will get him to open the exit and swap me for the kid." Harry closed his eyes, a draught of cold air suddenly ran down his spine he then spoke, "my, Daisy it's a great idea." Harry turned to Ryan and said, "what you think?" Ryan smiled and replied, "yeah Daisy it's a diamond."

Ryan removed the handcuffs, he then got out the shotgun from the boot. Daisy stretched out her arms and said, "okay Harry give me your mobile I promise no funny business." Harry looked her in the eyes and said, "that's good doll, I don't want to have to shoot you." Daisy smiled and said, "I know Harry you're all heart, a real gentleman."

Harry handed Daisy his mobile, she slowly began to dial Peter's number. Peter then heard his mobile ring out he reached inside his pocket and then answered the call. "Hi, Peter don't say anything just listen to what I have to say." Peter stood motionless and confused. "right! where do I start? Harry and Ryan have kidnapped me, Harry has informed me he will shoot me if you do not cooperate. bring the kid to the fire exit in exchange for me, tell the other two there are a couple of cops out front that will keep them busy do you understand everything I have said?"

Peter replied, "yes Daisy." then said, "right Peter see if you can sneak the kid out in the next five minutes do you understand?" Peter replied, "okay Daisy." Peter hung up, Macko looked to Peter with a puzzled face he then spoke in a deep voice, "what has happened to Daisy?" Peter replied, "oh she said there is a couple of cops out front that's why she hasn't returned yet."

Macko turned to Boris and said, "I reckon we need to take a look, Macko walked over to his holdall he then slowly opened it up and reached inside, his face produced a sinister smile. first, he pulled out two semi-automatic pistols, he placed each of them inside his belt and then his ultimate weapon, he lifted out an M16 automatic rifle complete with a grenade launcher.

He then filled his pockets with grenades and magazine clips. Boris smiled and said, "my, that's one mean weapon it's like the one-off that gangster movie Scarface." Macko agreed with a nod of his head he then said, "that's the one, say hello to my little friend." Macko opened a side pocket and produced a box, inside it, a syringe. Macko gritted his teeth and injected himself with the drug. Macko flexed his biceps he spoke in a deep voice, "my, I feel invincible. Boris let's do this."

They both walked over to the front of the warehouse, Harry, Ryan and Daisy made their way to the back of the warehouse. Harry felt distant, he looked up to a strange cloud formation, he then felt a cool breeze on the back of his neck. Ryan laughed he then said, "Harry you got your head in the clouds again." Harry shook his head he looked to Daisy and spoke, "what's keeping him?" Daisy replied, "oh remember I said to Peter the two cops out in the front? I am sorry guys, but I reckon your mates are about to get wasted."

James felt uneasy and called for backup. Macko caught sight of Rob, he smiled and became hysterical. Peter picked up the holdall with the money in it he then looked to David and said, "come on kid we are getting out of here before all hell breaks loose."

Peter escorted David to the fire exit and then the sound of Macko's assault rifle echoed all around. Macko had stepped outside and opened fire on Rob and James, they both died under the spray of bullets. Boris stepped back into the warehouse, he turned as he heard the exit door opening, he watched as Peter escorted David out. Boris lost his cool, he was not about to be double-crossed. he ran towards Peter and called out his name.

Harry grabbed hold of David pulling him out of the line of fire without warning Boris erupted like a volcano, he opened fire, several bullets hit Peter as he tried to escape. Daisy looked down at his lifeless body, she picked up the bag with the money in it, she became gripped by a hot flush panic. with wild strength, she struggled to escape.

The backup arrived in the shape of two patrol cars, they drove towards Macko who opened fire shooting a patrol car's driver and then the passenger died in a hail of bullets. a red mist had descended. Macko was intoxicated by violence, he then turned his attention to the second car launching a grenade. the car was engulfed by flames, the explosion echoed for miles. Boris then moved in for the kill, firing again and again.

Harry looked at Ryan, as Daisy took a bullet to her larynx and then another hit her in the temple. Ryan returned fire, his anger suddenly rose he then shouted, "God damn you!" as Boris stepped back inside the warehouse.

Ryan entered the warehouse; the crack of his shotgun echoed all around. Harry stood motionless, the words self-preservation entered his mind, he picked up the bag and then turned and moved swiftly away holding onto David's arm. Ryan took aim and shot Boris in the stomach, he stood bewildered gazing down, his heart was pounding, blood began to pour from the wound. Boris raised his weapon as Ryan shot him again in the chest. Boris fell to the ground letting off a shot which caught Ryan in the leg. Ryan fell backwards to the ground and cried out in pain. as Boris lay dead Ryan shouted, "out Harry's name, but to no avail.

a police helicopter was now hovering overhead watching over the carnage, his assistant called for backup as more and more patrol cars arrived Macko continued his onslaught, firing at every patrol car. the body count mounted up until the order was given to retreat by this time the scene resembled a war zone.

The chief of police gave the order, "Leave this one for Feds." Macko has now bathed in sweat his eyes were wild with madness. Harry rushed over to his car panic fears fluttered his mind. David looked up at Harry and spoke, "Your friend Ryan is wounded he has been shot in the leg, you must go back and save him before it is too late."

Harry gazed into David's eyes; anxiety twisted his face as he had a macabre vision of his wounded friend. Harry became very nervous; he reflected a shade of terror and then he expressed annoyance. "kid get in the car, better still get in the boot out of sight out of mind, I ain't going back to be shot."

Harry opened the boot and David climbed in. Harry put the bag with the money in the boot he then said, "okay kid stay quiet I aim to get us both out of here." Harry sat down and then without hesitation he put in the key into the ignition and hit the gas pedal driving away from the warehouse. David lay motionless rooted with fear. Harry looked ahead as panic fears fluttered his mind. he soon came to a halt at the roadblock, he was approached by two Police officers he wound down his window and produced his identity badge. one of the offices a tall man in his late forties spoke in a deep voice, "Hi I am Sergeant Bronson and your badge says your agent Harry. you have come from the direction of the shoot out were you involved did you see the kid?"

Harry replied, "no I didn't see any kid, my partner Ryan is inside the warehouse, he's wounded he took a bullet to the leg." the Sergeant looked into Harry's eyes with a sense of horror he then spoke, "Oh come, you fled and left your buddy?" Harry became very nervous, sweating furiously and then he became hysterical he then replied, " you, what you calling me a coward? would you stand and fight against machine gun Macko?" the Sergeant looked to his fellow officer and shook his head he then replied, " sorry Harry you're right, that guy is a stone-cold killer, up to now he's killed and wounded over a dozen officers. I will inform the feds about your wounded partner."

Harry regained his composure he then said, "yeah nice one, I must be getting back to relay my report." Sergeant Bronson stood back and signaled to the roadblock to let Harry past. Harry once more hit the gas pedal and pulled off at a slow pace.

Macko returned inside the warehouse as the police presence increased, more helicopters arrived. Ryan lay motionless pretending to be dead. Macko looked to his fallen comrade, Boris. he shook his head as he gazed, the fire exit door this has horror beyond imagination, all of his friends lay dead. a sound then echoed around the warehouse, "surrender! come out with your hands up, you're completely surrounded."

inspector Francis and Sergeant Canter arrived at the scene. the Inspector scanned all around at the various activities, he made enquiries about the siege he spoke to a Sergeant Bishop. "you say held up in the warehouse is machine gun Macko? has he any hostages?" "We believe there was a shootout inside the warehouse, there are dead bodies by the exit, a male and female."

the Inspector turned to his Sergeant and said, "could David be in the warehouse.? Sergeant Canter looked to sergeant Bishop and said, "any word on the two CIA Agents Harry and Ryan?" Sergeant Bishop replied, "oh I just heard from Sergeant Bronson, he informed me Harry left the scene. his friend Ryan was not so lucky, we believe he is in the warehouse wounded in the shootout."

the Inspector stood thinking for a while he then turned to Sergeant Bishop, "the kidnapped boy, David I believe Harry has fled the scene with the boy, he is very valuable to our country. do you understand?" Sergeant Bishop replied, "look, Inspector, the siege comes first, I got a complete madman ready to shoot anything or anyone that moves."

the Inspector agreed with a nod of his head he then spoke, "alright Sergeant we will be on our way." the Inspector then spoke to an FBI agent about David's kidnapping. "I believe Harry took the boy when he fled the scene." the FBI agent then said, "alright Inspector Francis we will track him down."

the Inspector smiled and then spoke in a calm voice, "good now we are getting somewhere." Inspector Francis and Sergeant Canter left accompanied by the FBI agent.

in the warehouse, Macko looked in disbelief, one minute he was promised twenty-five million and then this! a dream to a nightmare. he closed the exit door; he knew he was completely surrounded he noticed two drums of oil in the far corner of the warehouse. Macko took several steps back and then opened fire on the drums, an explosion and then flames that began to engulf the far corner of the warehouse.

Ryan knew he had to escape the madness; he began to crawl towards the entrance. Macko noticed Ryan crawling, his mind whispered" must have been playing the dead man." he then became angry he shouted, "die slug." his voice echoed all around the warehouse.

he then opened fire, Ryan never stood a chance and died in a hail of bullets. The swat team was now in place, two snipers awaited Macko. he knew it was end game time to die. Macko appeared at the entrance once more, he opened fire at anything that moved. the snipers took aim and shot Macko. he fell to his knees, blood pouring from a head and chest wound. several more bullets hit Macko and then he lay dead.

David closed his eyes; he had just witnessed the final shootout in his mind's eye out of the darkness came light. Cavoc appeared in David's mind, he whispered "judgement, very soon your ordeal will be over, it was your destiny to be kidnapped and brought to this country of sin. something you cannot alter, or defeat is your destiny, I promise you will soon be back in France with your loved ones and all of this will be a distant picture, David. after all of this is over, I will once more visit you in the land of dreams. I have so many stories to tell. David Burns had a wife by the name of Bella, she bore a son, she also named him David and the bloodline continued. I fear evil is eating away at your world. mankind with its greed will destroy this planet and the people on it. I fear all of this will come to an end."

David spoke with fear in his words, "but Cavoc, I don't want to witness the end of the world can I help?" Cavoc replied, "well then it's up to you to do something about it. your powers will grow and grow, in ten years' time your powers will bring about change to the planet Earth, the people will rejoice and obey whatever you say, wisdom shall be your way, you, David Trump, you are truly of David Burn's bloodline, a gift to alter the destiny of your Earth or put it on hold.

eventually, man will kill everything including this Planet. Since the days I visited your domain as a shapeshifter the wildlife has declined, human activity, climate change, mankind's greed poaching, overfishing, greenhouse gases produced by human activities. Undeveloped, uneducated countries such as Africa and India, the population will rise by billions, thus the food will run out. I see millions dead due to global warming disaster after disaster. I must go now, remember you have nothing to lose, no one shall harm you."

Cavoc began to fade from David's mind and then darkness returned. Harry pulled over parking his Cadillac at the back of a small Hotel. David opened his eyes the words of Cavoc flashed through his mind. Harry appeared, he opened the boot and then light. Harry then whispered, "okay kid a lot of good people have died this day so if you don't pick out the jackpot winning numbers you will be joining them, do I make myself clear?" David replied, "crystal clear."

Harry then said, "good that's what I wanted to hear, now let's get you a drink and a bite to eat. time is my biggest enemy I am simply running out of time."

Harry booked the two of them into a room, he also made an order to have some food and drinks delivered to the room. they both entered as Harry unlocked the door. it was a small room that served its purpose. Harry turned to David he had an uneasy feeling he then spoke in a calm voice, "David I want you to sit down and watch the television whilst I have a quick wash, the food and drink will be here in a minute."

David focused on Harry and then spoke, "I can't wait I am starving." Harry entered the bathroom whilst

David turned on the television and sat down. Harry looked to his worst enemy, the mirror. anxiety twisted his face, a strong sense of compulsion, he then began to talk to himself. "well Harry here's another fine mess you got me into how you are going to get out of this?"

Harry turned on the tap he began to splash water on his face, he then reached for a towel, wiping away the water, Harry stood motionless. if only he could turn back the clock. Harry then heard a knock on the door. the food and drinks had arrived.

Harry rushed towards the door, opening it with anticipation, a very large bearded man stood before him complete with a large bag. he then spoke with a distant strange accent. "hi buddy, got your order here." Harry put on a polite smile and paid the delivery man. he then took the bag and closed the door with great haste.

Harry then said, "okay kid I got you your burger and fries and a cola." Harry handed David the food and drink. David finally got his burger and fries, he smiled with content. the FBI searched for Harry; Inspector Francis sat talking to agent Smith. "I believe Harry has David."

in a low-profile hotel, agent Smith mustered a confident smile and then spoke, "I believe you could be right; we will concentrate all our resources on searching all of the hotels in the area." The Inspector then spoke in a deep voice, "I believe Harry is a creature of habit, he will be asking David to pick out the winning numbers on the lottery."

Smith's eyes perked with curiosity, he shook head and then spoke in a voice of disbelief. "Inspector Francis that's just not possible is it?" the Inspector replied, "Oh but it is, the boy has powers beyond our comprehension. we need to find this boy as quickly as possible, if I am correct my greatest fear is David may hold back and not predict the correct numbers."

back at the hotel, it was now late in the evening, Harry began to yawn and then a voice in his head cried out for his bed. he then turned his attention to David, blinking and frowning, he then spoke, "okay kid get yourself some shuteye, it's been a long day. you have the bed, I will sleep here, and no funny business! don't try to escape."

David smiled and replied, "Harry, I am going nowhere, all of this will soon be over." Harry shook his head and then spoke, "My, you're a confident kid, oh I forget you predict the future. just get in there and go to sleep." David did what Harry said, and they both went to sleep."

the following day, Harry woke David up and then said, "get out of bed." David got out of bed and followed Harry. they then sat down. Harry looked to David he then spoke with a shade of impatience, "right kid, now to business. I want you to write down the lottery numbers, it takes place in eight hours."

David listened to Harry's words; something did not add up. Harry, a wanted man now, however, would he be able to collect the winnings. David began to read Harry's mind; his secret wasn't safe. a thought flashed through Harry's brain he then voiced his concerns, "my God! you just read my mind, didn't you?"

David was honest, he did not know how to lie, he then replied, "you're right, I can read your mind, I know all about Robert, your distant cousin, he has agreed to lie for you and pick up the winnings."

Harry reflected a shade of horror he then spoke, "kid that information you did not need to know about, okay what I am thinking now kid?" David sat rooted with fear; his heart began to pound. Harry suddenly burst into laughter he then spoke, "kid I am only messing with your head, I wouldn't harm you. I aim to hide you away until I've got my hands on the money, I imagine you would spill the beans on my little plan."

David sat silent, "so I am right, maybe some of your powers are rubbing off on me, anyway, kid the quicker we get this done the better. you will be back with your parents. what the hell! I will even pay for the flight home, eight hundred dollars, let's hurry."

Harry located a pen and a piece of paper and then he handed them to David. he then said, "okay kid concentrate, I am gonna take a look at the time whilst you pick out the winning numbers." David sat, he closed his eyes and slipped into a trance-like state. numbers began to occupy his mind; he then imagined the lottery draw. he slowly began to write down the numbers until he had completed the task.

Harry reappeared and then spoke in a confident voice, "okay kid have you picked out the winning numbers?" with a confident smile David replied, "yes Harry, here are the numbers you require to win the lottery." Harry then said, "well-done, let's get these numbers on and you will soon be back in France."

David stood up and followed Harry out of the hotel. they both walked over to the car park and then onto the Cadillac. Harry opened up the boot, he then opened up the holdall it was full of dollars. he closed it and then turned to David and said, "it's for your own good, I am too close to the jackpot, I can't afford to get caught."

David hesitated for a brief second a voice in his head said, "very soon this will all be over." David climbed into the boot, he lay down and closed his eyes. Harry shut the boot with a bang which echoed in David's ears. Harry started up his car moving of slowly his mind whispered "jackpot".

the sun shone and then it was replaced with clouds, and rain started to patter against his window screen. Harry drove a short distance until he arrived at a store selling lottery tickets. Harry parked his car out of sight and then made his way to the store. the rain had come to a halt.

Harry looked up at the strange cloud formations, he then took a deep breath as he entered the store Harry's mind whispered "this is the big one play it cool" Harry pulled out the piece of paper from deep inside his pocket this was his time he filled in the lottery ticket checking and rechecking he had written the right numbers down. gradually Harry ventured towards the shop assistant over anticipation ran high. Harry forced a smile and then spoke with confidence. "I would like to put on my lottery for this evening draw." the store assistant was a tall female redhead complete with gleaming teeth. she nodded her head and then spoke in a quiet voice, "Alright sir, I will put it on for you."

Harry handed the ticket to the assistant along with a ten-dollar bill. the assistant smiled and handed Harry the lottery ticket and his change. Harry's impossible mission had been accomplished. the relief was the order of the day. Harry placed the ticket and his change into his pocket and made his way towards the exit door.

Inspector Francis asked for an update from Agent Smith. "well, Inspector Francis, as we speak there are patrol cars visiting all stores that sell lottery tickets, it is but a matter of time before we apprehend Harry and you get your boy back."

Inspector Francis then spoke in a deep voice, "good, I wish I was so confident Agent Smith, the draw will take place in thirty minutes, could we not join in the search for him?" Agent Smith replied, "why yes, but remember Harry is a very dangerous man, my officers will shoot him as long as David isn't caught up in the crossfire, I give you my word you and David will soon be on a flight back to France."

Inspector Francis then said, "good, the sooner the better." Agent Smith began to laugh "okay" he then said, "let us go." they were soon joined by Sergeant Canter and Agent Daniels.

all four men left the building and walked to where Agent Smith's car was parked up. after a brief conversation, they were back searching the streets for Harry and David. Harry had returned to the car, he sat thinking of Daisy and Ryan. the order of the day, death and decay.

Harry began to sweat furiously, his heart began to pound until he opened his eyes, a man stood next to his car, a regular gutter punk. he stood looking straight at the car. Harry grew hysterical a voice in his head said, "stay calm." the gutter punk was conscious of Harry's annoyance but just didn't care. he has dressed in rags, black busy hair and discoloured skin.

Harry pulled out his pistol and pointed it towards the gutter punk with eyes of extreme terror the gutter punk turned and began to run for his life. Harry scanned all around and then re-holstered his weapon.

David had been visited by an angel. he continued to speak "I have often wondered why angels only visit certain people." the angel replied, "the reason for this is we give comfort and try to protect chosen individuals, enlightenment is the key. your wisdom will set you free, your destiny awaits the power. no one will defy you; you are the enlightened one. I must go now the evil one is approaching."

she disappeared and then the boot opened, it was Harry. he looked down at David and said, "okay their kid, do you need a drink and something to eat maybe a candy bar? the moment of truth is upon us, the lottery draw, let's hope for your sake it's a jackpot win, if not it's curtain's for you kid."

Harry shut the boot before David could say anything. a patrol car pulled up. Harry knew he had been recognised, he had come this far there was no going back, he couldn't do time he suddenly felt a red mist descending on him, he was leaking loads of perspiration.

Harry opened his car door and reached for the shotgun without warning he pointed it at the patrol car and started to shoot. the front window of the patrol car exploded.

Harry was now homicidal, again and again, he pumped bullets into the patrol car, the crack of the shotgun blast echoed all around until Harry was finished and the two Police Officers died instantly without a chance.

Harry's mind became paralysed by the hideous sight, suddenly he cried out "God damn you!" the streets came to life with the sound of the shotgun, people arrived on the scene. Harry got into his car and placed the shotgun down on the seat, he then hit the gas pedal. driving away from the scene of death at great speed.

David lay in the boot; he had heard the shots and lay frozen with fear. a Police helicopter flew overhead, the pilot followed Harry and reported his location. several Patrol cars were now on the tail of Harry. he looked in his wing mirror in disbelief, he became gripped with fear and then a wild cry of malice, "leave me alone!" Harry was reddened with rage; anxiety twisted his face.

Harry looked at his watch, five minutes until the draw. the Harry drove faster and faster, trying his best to evade the pursuing patrol cars. more and more arrived on the scene. Agent Smith looked to Inspector Francis and said, "have you any thoughts on the pursuit?" the Inspector replied, "yes Agent Smith I have a plan. inform the pursuing patrol cars to keep a tail on Harry, but he must be given a wide birth." I believe he will head for the first store he comes across, we could be waiting for him there, I have a gut feeling David is locked in the boot of his car, we would be better off taking him out when he is parked up away from David. could you call off the pursuit slowly and we need an element of surprise."

Agent Smith with his usual composure agreed with Inspector Francis. Agent smith called off the pursuit, the cars began to fade away from the pursuit. Inspector Francis smiled and said, "I am convinced all of this will soon be over how many stores are there near to where he is travelling?"

"the draw has taken place, one hundred million dollars, it's strange he must be a mad man how on earth does he expect to collect the money?" Agent Smith with his usual cool and calm composure replied, "you're right, I believe he has no intention of collecting the money himself, maybe he has contacted someone and given them the numbers, or maybe he opted for a smaller win of which he could collect. Yes, perhaps."

"I believe he went completely mad killing two police officers, that makes him even more dangerous does it not?" Agent Daniels looked at a map whilst Agent Smith contacted the police helicopter that was still pursuing Harry. he asked for a location and then pulled off towards Harry.

he began frowning in confusion, the Patrol Cars were called off, he had a bewildered look about him the radiant sun shone down on him, Harry's mouth was dry, and he was sweating. Harry made a sharp turn and drove towards the nearest store. Harry was oblivious to the helicopter hovering overhead. an FBI agent was parked up near the store, he looked into his mirror and could not believe his eyes. it was Harry's car. he watched as Harry parked up next to the store, the agent contacted Agent Smith and informed him of Harry's location. Agent Smith put his foot down on the gas pedal heading towards the store.

Agent Daniels alerted agents from miles around to converge on Harry, including swat teams. Harry scanned all around and then picked up his shotgun, he opened up the glove compartment and reached for his spare ammunition. he reloaded his shotgun, he was now bathed in sweat, thoughts of doom flushed his mind.

Harry climbed out of his car and moved gingerly towards the store complete with shotgun. Harry took a deep breath then entered the store, a couple of shoppers took one look at Harry with his shotgun and decided to exit the store. a store assistant looked to Harry in confusion, she had long hair tied back in a ponytail, rolled up sleeves and a square forehead.

Harry then spoke in a deep voice, "okay lady I am a CIA agent, get me the lottery results now." he talked with a shade of impatience in his voice, the assistant agreed with a feeling of unease. Harry walked over to the fridge and helped himself to a beer, he removed the screw cap and began to drink the cold beer.

Harry did not realise he was now completely surrounded by swat teams and FBI Agents as he drank the ice-cold beer.

Inspector Francis arrived on the scene along with Sergeant Canter and the FBI agents Inspector Francis turned to Agent Smith and expressed his concerns. "Harry is in the store we must rescue David from the boot before Harry starts shooting." Agent Smith contacted the swat team who raced towards the car, they opened the boot by force and rescued David."

at last, an agent lifted David out of the boot. he then shut it. the agent smiled and said, "you're safe now kid your ordeal is over." David's heart was pounding and then a comforting sense of relief.

Harry finished off the bottle of beer and then looked to the store assistant and said, "okay where are my numbers?" Harry put his shotgun on a shelf and then produced the ticket from deep inside his pocket. the store assistant handed Harry a piece of paper with the results on it. Harry took a deep breath, his mind whispered "judgement".

with total concentration Harry began to check the numbers, the first number five, the next number eight, and then number seventeen, followed by number thirty-three, and then things start to go wrong.

Harry looked at the ticket in total disbelief and then a sense of compulsion, again and again, he checked the numbers. suddenly his anger rose, "God damn you, David!" he cried, he then turned his attention to the store assistant "the results you have given me, they are correct, take my ticket I want to know how much money I have won."

the shop assistant checked how much Harry had won, she smiled "good news Sir you will be able to pay for your beer out of your winnings, you have won eight hundred dollars."

Harry's anger erupted like a volcano, he remembered the conversation, eight hundred dollars to get David a flight home to Paris. Harry picked up the shotgun, the store assistant reflected a shade of terror and ducked beneath the counter. Harry shouted out in a loud voice, "I am going to kill that kid."

a draught of cold air suddenly ran down his spine as he left the store, the words continued to ring in his mind. the flight home is eight hundred dollars. Harry was in a trance-like state he stepped out of the store oblivious to the Swat team and FBI Agents. the car boot of his car suddenly opened.

Harry gazed in disbelief; it was empty. Harry turned and scanned all around him he could see all of the weapons trained upon him. he mumbled "end game." as he lifted up his shotgun. before he could fire the Swat, team opened fire semi-automatic rounds hit Harry from every direction, he died in a hail of bullets. he fell to the ground and lay dead motionless. it was all over.

Inspector Francis put his arm around David as tears came to his eyes, "this was a harsh lesson, he had learned the cruel reality of mankind. the Inspector and Sergeant Canter escorted David back to Paris where he was reunited with his family.

Author's Note.

I have always enjoyed writing and started off with poetry. I became a member of the poetry society I completed over five hundred poems on a variety of subjects. I then became a member of the guild of international songwriters and composers. I have always been a prolific writer and have a vast collection of poems and short stories. My completed poems have been published in The Standard newspaper for the last twenty years.

I often had people contacting me telling me how much they enjoyed my poems. Some of the poems I wrote to my total amazement predicted future events. I believe we all have a degree of psychic potential that lies dormant until it is activated. I have experienced such potential over the past years I remember having a vision of a helicopter crashing, I then turned on the television to find it breaking news. Another example is when I think of someone I haven't heard of for a long time and minutes later they contact me.

I often listen to music and on lots of occasions I have thought of a song I haven't heard in a long time; I would turn on the radio and the song will be playing or about to be played. I remember many years ago riding to work on a bicycle with a friend, I told him I had a vision about being crushed by steel. After work, we were riding home when a heavy goods vehicle loaded with steel pulled out in front of us the driver hit his brakes just missing us.

My story 'Five Fives Beyond Imagination' came to me in a series of visions unlocking the mysteries that have haunted mankind throughout the centuries. I believe in the power of numerology. Numbers compose the very foundation of reality; throughout the centuries people have believed it is possible to predict the future.

I have studied numerology for many years, it is based on the belief numbers are not solid but vibrations and energies that move. Vibrations influence our lives with either the dark shadow side negative experiences; separation or light positive experiences connection.

Your destiny can be determined using numerology. Philosopher, Pythagoras studied numerology, he believed as I do, numbers are the essence of life. I was born in October my collective year which shows my qualities are bringing wisdom to the world. My personal year table is the number five which represents communication each number contains emotional, mental, physical and spiritual dimensions this is why numerology is such an amazing representation of life.

The basis of numerology is that we are influenced by our birth name and our birthdate, the numbers five and eight have influenced me throughout my life. An example of this is in 2014 I had two accidents, I added the date and the month together and came up with the numbers five and eight, throughout my life I have lived at number five or eight. I believe when these numbers clash my luck turns bad as together these numbers add up to thirteen.

I mentioned earlier about my poems, some of which predicted future events. I remember gazing at the front of a newspaper at the sad face of Princess Diana, I put pen to paper and wrote a poem about the Princess in the summer of nineteen ninety- seven, recalling the end of the poem " life goes fast when you are harassed, you sealed your fate when you made that date, don't cry Di it wasn't meant to be" Two months later she went on a date with Dodi and they were harassed by the paparazzi and they both died under tragic circumstances.

Another strange thing that happened to me when I was moving autographed pictures in my bar room in the summer of two thousand and three, I have got over a dozen pictures, I placed them on the floor, all of a sudden, I noticed a large fly sitting on the face of Charles Bronson. I chased the fly away only for it to return to the same spot. Later, I found out that Charles Bronson had died.

In two thousand and three, I sat watching the movie, The Bodyguard, later on about midnight, I picked out a random episode of an eighties show entitled Thriller, the episode I put on was about a killer who would meet women and then drown them in their bathtubs. Later on, I heard the news about Whitney Houston who also died in a bathtub.

In the past, I have had dreams about celebrities and then the following morning turned on the news to find out they had passed away. I have read, prediction is very difficult especially about the future. I once worked at a large warehouse that employed hundreds, the canteen staff started a weekly raffle each week I would buy one strip of five tickets. I won nine weeks on the run, prizes such as a £100 hamper. The bizarre thing was I would write on the back of the ticket this is the winning ticket before the draw and that ticket would win the prize.

I visited a local social club which was full of people buying raffle tickets, I bought a strip of five tickets and the draw took place I won the first prize and then was invited to pick the next ticket. I picked out my own ticket even though the bucket was full of tickets. I won again, someone else then picked the third and fourth tickets I won all four prizes with five tickets.

I remember the faces around the club as I won all four prizes, people began to shout "fix" as what I had done was impossible. I became so confident believing I just couldn't lose, a friend asked me to go for a drink and I agreed, we went out to a local pub, inside the pub they were selling raffle tickets for a cash prize. I informed my friend that I would buy some tickets and that later we should return, and I would give him half the money. We returned later, as usual, I wasn't disappointed. I kept my word and gave my friend half the money.

On another occasion, a friend told me he had never won anything in his life, we entered a pub selling raffle tickets for a meat hamper. I informed my friend that if he were to go up and buy a ticket, he would win the hamper. He agreed, and to his total amazement, he won for the first time in his life.

I expected to win every time and did so. I remember entering a pub, buying some raffle tickets, I never won first prize, so I ripped up the tickets in disbelief. I had to put the tickets back together as it was unknown to me there was a second prize and I had won it.

I had a bizarre winning streak that continued for many years, then I started filling in a pools coupon. I started off eight to eleven weeks later I changed to eight to ten, what a mistake. I had accidentally put an extra cross on the winning line that would have won me a small fortune.

The company in question sent me a cheque for a sum in good faith. I remember thinking to myself perhaps I wasn't destined to win such a large sum of money. My lucky and unlucky numbers have always been five and eight. These two numbers have always played a part in my life. I used the same numbers on the EuroMillions, the week I never used them they came in fourteen million. I would have won, I found out I had all the winning numbers except five and eight. I believe eventually I will win pick out the correct winning numbers.

I remember visiting a supermarket several times and guessing the correct price of the shopping without adding it up. I informed the lady on the till how much it would be before she started to scan the items and I was correct she looked at me and said, "I bet you couldn't do that again." I informed her that I had already guessed the correct price of shopping on multiple occasions.

In 2003 I was driving to the town centre and had a vision of a woman stepping out onto the road in front of a car. I returned home and began to write down my vision, it was my first short story. Every day I wrote more short stories, I was once in bed after working a night shift, I could see characters and a story unfolding I knew that if I didn't write the story onto paper, I wouldn't be able to sleep. I sat up and then picked up a pen and a large notepad, I began writing at a prolific pace and found myself in a trance-like state.

I wrote nonstop for over one hour and when the story was completed. I just looked at the number of pages in amazement. I had written a complete short story entitled "Wits About" It was truly an amazing horror story.

I remember competing in the Great North Run, I had a vision of a young man wanting to compete in the London Marathon, his father was a gangster controlling the North of England, he eventually grants his son permission to run the marathon as long as he had a trusted bodyguard.

Things go wrong in the south, and then all hell breaks loose between the north and the south. This is probably the best gangster story ever written, full of twists and gang warfare. As with all the short stories I have written I can picture the characters as though I was watching a movie, the ideas I had for my short stories are all original.

I was the most prolific in the year two thousand and three, a short story entitled "The Judgement" "Angels and Demons" and then a science fiction story.

several years later I bought a DVD called "The knowing" I watched this movie in total disbelief, the story was about a professor, John predicting future disasters. The short story I had written was very similar to this movie which I had written in two thousand and three. The main character in this story was a professor, John.

I continued to write more and more stories and only on one occasion, I have stopped writing halfway through a story as it was the most frightening story. I mentioned earlier I could see all the characters and the surroundings as I was on a film set, the story was about the supernatural.

Imagine being on the film set of the most frightening film ever made. This is the reason I stopped writing and switched to another story. I sent off a thriller to the BBC and various publishers I believe this was a mistake on my behalf, I remember thinking I have over five hundred short stories I just wanted feedback.

One of the first stories I wrote after the millennium was entitled "Five fives beyond imagination" I had a vision of David Burns travelling to the fifth dimension to meet Cavoc. Later I decided to write Nostradamus into my story every time I wrote fiction. Later on, I researched and found it to be a fact.

For instance, I wrote Nostradamus was in Montpellier on a certain date and John Dee in Paris on another date, to my amazement, fiction turned to fact as they were there on those dates.

I finished the story whilst cruising around the Caribbean. In the same year, I also went to Ibiza, the night-time entertainment at the hotel was poor, my son, Bradley asked me to play cards, I hadn't played for a while and soon ran out of games. He then said, "I will shuffle the pack and you have to pick out the ten of diamonds. I have no knowledge of card tricks but picked out the correct card until I had picked out all of the tens, impossible I thought.

My daughter, Shanna had made friends with a group of teenagers that all looked like characters out of the Harry Potter movie. One, in particular, informed me he could do card tricks, I carried on picking out all the Kings. People began to look in amazement, I soon had an audience. The Harry Potter lookalike examined the deck and then shuffled it several times he then said, "Okay pick out the Queen of Spades."

I concentrated on the deck of cards and then to everyone's amazement I picked out the correct card, I remember his shocked face and his words "My God how on Earth did you do that?" I cannot explain how I picked out all the correct cards, but the word 'impossible' had no meaning to me.

I signed the contract to have "Five fives beyond imagination" published on 31.10.14. I have been contacted by various famous American authors, one sent me a message reading "your book isn't good, it's great I've just read it hurry up and publish another one and I will buy it".

I also had a message from an American author who explained she kept having visions of "Five fives". She then mentioned the fall, 2014 about the time I signed the contract to have it published. This was such an enlightening year. Forty-four days later on the 14.12.2014, I lay in bed dreaming about my book, then I felt a strange presence in the room. I suddenly opened my eyes and sat up, I turned to the right and there stood before me, were two angels. I gazed upon them mesmerised by their radiant beauty. I could not take my eyes off them.

I remember their smiling faces, such a hypnotizing display. My eyes suddenly flickered spasmodically and then they faded away. I was so confused why visit me on this date? Bewildered, I could see in my mind's eye their tender looks and glowing faces.

One month later I uncharacteristically decided to tidy out some old letters, and then I found the answer I was looking for. A letter from a solicitor dating back to 14.12.10, this was the date of an accident I had whilst driving towards a roundabout. I stopped to give way to the traffic when a large van crashed into the back of me, the driver was going too fast and never hit his brakes in time. The van pushed me onto the roundabout, somehow,

I managed to steer my car to the left avoiding other traffic. I suffered whiplash but believe it could have been a lot worse. The angels visited me on the anniversary of the accident four years to the day. I believe in the impossible and that I was visited by two guardian angels.

Ten days later I dreamt of the number 347 again and again as if this was some sort of message. I have been predicting future events all my life but was not prepared for what awaited me when I visited Chester to be interviewed by a reporter from The Standard newspaper.

The date was 13.5.15, I parked outside Chester and then walked to the Standard office. I met the reporter who asked me "Why did you start writing?" I explained to her in 2003 I was driving along and then had a vision of a young lady stepping out in front of a car. I returned home and wrote a short story about the vision. After that I had visions and dreams on a regular basis, this is how I wrote five hundred original remarkable short stories, anyone I could expand into a book.

Imagine horror, thrillers ec.t I consider them to be priceless. I finished the interview then visited the Bluebell Inn which was featured in my book. The manager gave me a guided tour of the Inn this was the oldest inn in Chester. I remember thinking as a draught of cold air ran down my spine this place is spooky. I then walked around Chester handing out leaflets advertising my book for some strange reason people kept asking me the same question over and over again, "Why did you start writing?"

I then noticed the time had flown by. It was time to leave Chester. For some reason the subway was closed so I made my way to St Oswald's, the road was very busy, I gazed all around and noticed two Asian men walking towards the traffic lights, and then my attention turned to a young lady in her late twenties she was speed walking with a very small dog on a lead.

She was dressed in a light pink and green vest and matching shorts. I gazed over at her, my mind was saying get across the road as quickly as possible. I noticed a break in the traffic and without hesitation, I jogged across the road if I had not, I would have stood next to the young lady waiting for the lights to change. I crossed the road and as I went to walk away, I heard a loud bang I turned around, gazed in shock and horror at the young lady who had been hit by a blue Peugeot 307 this happened at approximately 15;31

I stood frozen gazing at her motionless body; I remember the small dog stepping over her body. More and more people arrived on the scene and within minutes the Police arrived and then the Ambulance service. She was at the lights by herself, my mind whispered you could have maybe prevented her from crossing, or you could have shared her fate. The answer to this question I will never know had the vision in 2003 finally come true?

A reporter from the Ellesmere Port Pioneer was also doing a story on me, he informed me if he needed anything else, he would contact me.

Two weeks later I contacted him and asked him if he required anything else for the story, a brief silence and then he replied, in a shocked voice, "My, that is very spooky, I have just finished your story and was about to contact you to see if you had a brighter photograph. I then informed him, spooky is something I had always done.

I am friends on Facebook with a lot of award-winning authors, one, in particular, an award-winning Canadian author contacted me with a message which read 'I believe you are interested in Numerology, do you know the Bible code number? it took boffins with the aid of computers to come up with the answer which was the number seven." I replied to her that I had come to the same conclusion with the aid of a pen and a piece of paper just after the Millennium.

I remember it was Easter, I sat watching three Biblical movies back to back. Later on, I started to apply some deep thought about the movies I had just watched, three words came to me, Jesus, cross and Gospel. I then applied Numerology, each word when added up came to the same number 74. I then thought of the Bible which was 30. So, I then timed $3 \times 74 = 222$ and then $3 \times 222 = 666$. I then looked into the 74 words spelt out GD, the Bible 30 using the 0 it spelt out GOD, I then found out one more word Jewish which was 74 so I timed $4 \times 74 = 296$ which spelt out BIF spelt backwards it spelt out FIB.

I then noticed two words, Baptist and Priest both came to the number 87 timed by two $2 \times 87 = 174$ GD.

I believe numbers are the key to unlocking the mysteries of the universe. The bible code number seven is one of the most significant numbers because of its spiritual perfection. Oh, such hidden messages and meanings of codes.

Christians believe seven to be a holy number. Genesis says that God rested on the seventh day and that mankind was created on the sixth. There are seven continents, seven ocean's, seven heavens, seven colours in the rainbow, seven wonders of the world and seven days a week and so on. Indeed, number seven is truly extraordinary. It is also written the number seven is of spiritual enlightenment, inner-wisdom pure energy of the mystics. It is related to my star sign, libra's psychic abilities are also mentioned.

The award-winning Canadian author contacted me about the bible code number seven as I was about to go on holiday to Majorca. Seven letters I printed off my boarding pass only to find out I was sitting on seat seven. I arrived at my hotel and the room number added up to seven. I often went on holidays by myself so I could chill out in the sun and write a book. I sat next to a lady and her husband the lady asked me if I was an author I replied, "yes."

I informed her I was writing my second book and my first one had just been published. She then said she was a speed reader complete with a very high IQ. She then informed me how she would love to read my published book, I lent her a copy to read. She thanked me and began to read, her eyes lit up, wide-eyed she read on and suddenly stopped. She was a tall lady and possessed such appealing beauty. She turned to me with an expression of amazement and said, "How on earth did you think of this?"

The lady was hooked on the story, she continued to read. Later on, she kept tight hold of the book as if it was a rare treasure. She then said, "name your price I will pay anything for this book as I want to read it again and again." She then handed me twenty Euros. The entertainment team then appeared and asked me to roll two giant dice I got a four and a three.

All through the holiday the number seven kept coming to me in some shape or form. It was now time to leave. I travelled to Palma de Mallorca airport it was very large and busy with nearly twenty million passengers using this airport a year. I approached a group of strangers and asked them a question about the check out as I couldn't find it.

The group informed me we're to go for the flight to Manchester. Later on, I saw them in a different queue checking in to the flight. I then ended up in a seat next to them, imagine the odds on this happening.

I arrived home and later visited a cool trader store, I brought various items and the old lady on the till said, "that's strange seven pounds seventy-seven pence." I remember attending a local street party me and my son, Bradley played football with a couple of Police constables, they then brought raffle tickets and believed the prizes where outstanding. What could I say? I informed them of the will to win and that the prizes already had my name written on them.

I had done this for many years, I grew in confidence as the draw took place and wasn't disappointed, winning the first and second prizes, the luck of the draw was with me once more.

I remember being informed by someone that they never dream. I myself have had lots of dreams the Native American Indians considered dreams as an important source of information about future events, interpreting and understanding is the key to unlock your dreams.

There are many levels of existence happening at the same time, it is conceivable that dreams pick up material from other time frames or parallel realities that we are not aware of in our conscious World. My dreams are so vivid, some supernatural, providing information about future events. I have also had out of body dreams witnessing spiritual beings of light and darkness. Imagine flying through the clouds and then looking down on a natural disaster and then later turning on the television and finding out your dream had become reality.

Premonitions occur in the land of dreams because of time, it is different in the higher dimensions, the causal mechanism. This turns action from one place to another, the event witnessed in a dream later on it materializes in our domain.

Some people adopt a memory, trained to remember and write down the dates and description of such dreams of such examples yes, I have many I have picked out some of my favourites. The first was on 9.3.16, I dreamt I was walking along in a Latin American Country the radiant sun was shining in all of its glory. I looked up; trees filled with bananas. I then turned to someone and said, "the trees are blocking out the sun." and then total darkness.

The following day I turned on the television to watch the news. I then found out there had been a Solar Eclipse in the region I had dreamt of. The next dream was so vivid as are all of my dreams on the 24.3.16, I dreamt I was in America, riots broke out all over the country, so I then left on an aeroplane. For some reason, I lived in France near the Belgium border. My dwelling was an old farmhouse. I gazed out of the window awaiting a Nuclear explosion, the fallout destroyed everything in its path including me.

Days later I read about some terrorists that had planned to attack a nuclear plant in the area. I had dreamed of.

The next dream was on the 9.4.16, I remember two neighbours shooting at each other from their houses and then two elephants appeared and then two dinosaurs, was this a message of Mankind's extinction?

On the 11.4.16 I lay in bed dreaming of the Grand National, the dream then switched to a Baseball team of forty, everyone had to queue up to receive a number and sign their name. I signed my name and was given the number three, as soon as I signed my alarm clock went off. I got out of bed and then went downstairs and opened a cupboard and a loaf of opened bread fell out onto the worktop, only three pieces of bread fell out of the wrapper.

Soon after this I got into my car and turned on the radio the DJ then mentioned the number three. Three years later I checked the results only to find out the winner won with odds of thirty-three to one.

The next dream was on the 12.4.16, I was on a building site high up walking along a scaffolding I stopped and gazed over the edge, I put two hands on the rail which was not secure. I then fell over the edge. The following day I attended a risk assessment course. The course started off with a DVD with a man falling from scaffolding exactly the same as my dream.

The next dream was on the 10.6.16, I visited the Whitehouse to meet Donald Trump he revealed to me just like a coin, he had two sides, one good, one bad. He then informed me he was possessed by evil but was still a good man. Later I remember thinking, but Donald Trump is not in the Whitehouse. It was three months later when he was elected President.

The next dream on the 16.6.16 was very vivid and supernatural, aeroplanes were going missing they simply vanished from the sky in my dream they were being transported to a mystical dark realm. A giant demonic monster had amassed a graveyard of aeroplanes. Suddenly a new one appeared the monster began to rip open the cockpit with huge claws and supernatural strength. I could hear the passengers screaming, the monster began to feed. With every feed it became angrier, it then became larger and more insane.

The creature then stopped and announced it would travel to the dimension of the humans and feed at will. The creature could turn on an armour coating that could stop any weapon forged by mankind.

The next dream was on the 7.7.16, I dreamt I was walking along the streets in America watching events unfolding, suddenly large black stones hit the ground all around me, I then turned to see they were bullets. Later on, I read the story of the Dallas Police officers ambushed, twelve shot and five killed.

On the 8.9.16 I wrote a poem which began with the words "imagine as the dark nights draw in and the supernatural events begin." I went to bed and wasn't disappointed at 05;09 in the morning I felt a strange presence, I could not sleep and opened my eyes to see a face looking at me. The face was that of an 18th-century man I felt he was someone famous of that era. The face was in a circle all around it was golden flames I watched as it began to move across the bedroom, it then disappeared through the corner of the ceiling.

On the 9.9.16 I was visited by angels in the land of dreams. I then looked at the date of my first visit 14.12.15, if you takeaway 14 - 9, 12 - 9 and 15 - 16 you are left with the number nine.

On the 19.9.16 I had a nightmare it was so vivid, imagine a very old large mansion with lots of people living in it including a wicked Witch. I stood outside in the dream looking up to a top window she stood in a boarded-up room, she was dressed in a purple dress and a grey cardigan matching her grey hair. She hates children and was angry and frustrated as she could not find her scarf, she uses to strangle them.

The Witch would then made it look like an accident; her face was full of warts her eyes as dead as the night such a sinister sight. The Witch then found her scarf and began to kill the children one by one. My alarm clock did not go off at 05;30 for some reason instead it went off at 06;00.

Autumn is a time for the supernatural my next dream on the 13.10.16 was very enlightening a magical, beautiful dream which I believe was a message from beyond. I was looking through a magical giant book every time I turned a page over, I visited the country on the page. It was like an out of body experience an atmosphere of bliss and enchantment the book gave of such Heavenly light. The book revealed information about the different countries, cultures and population. I got to the last page and suddenly the magical light faded as it then revealed all the different countries' weapons of mass destruction. The dream was so magical, beyond words I feel lucky to have witnessed such a dream, the end message I believe was mankind will destroy itself with such weapons of mass destruction.

The next was on the 16.10.16, I dreamt I was watching the news and its coverage of America and its allies invading North Korea. I watched the sky filled with American bombers and then the tanks and infantry people all around me were expressing their horror. The War had just started and then the news reporter mentioned the death toll so far it read 16,000. The dream then switched to a giant tower block in our country, I stood outside watching a fire out of control. A person asked me to help the burning people inside I replied, "no" fearful for my own health and safety.

I remember just standing there watching people burn in the fire, was this another prediction of a future event? The following year the Grenfell fire, I dreamt of a tower burning on the 16. 10. 16 the tower burnt on the 14;6 take away 16 from 14 and 6 from 10 you are left with 24. Grenfell had 24 storeys

The next dream was amazing on the 7.1.17, in the land of dreams I was visited by angels and then taken to Heaven on a guided tour through the Pearly gates oh such majesty and enchantment the ultimate dream. I remember a feeling of ultimate bliss as the angels spoke with me, they explained to me how everything operates in great detail. I remember everything was so bright I was shown a queue of people awaiting passage to Heaven. I remember a giant set of scales I watched as they judged the next person in the queue, giving off such dazzling light. I was then informed they were the scales of Justice. If they turned dark, then it is below you go.

There was also a place between Heaven and Hell in which you could enhance a second chance. The deeds you declare some of which fair, the Angels will then decide upon your final ride. I cannot remember everything that happened in the dream, but the following day, I sat and then wrote a poem about my heavenly encounter.

The next dream was on the 15;3;17 I dreamt the president of Russia met up with the president of Turkey. Later on, they visited England and came to my house, they both entered and sat down talking whilst I made them a cup of tea each. All of a sudden, the dream switched to Turkey I was in a bar, I entered it and then noticed a man sitting alone upset drinking Vodka. I walked over to the man and asked him if everything was alright, he explained to me back in Russia he had fallen asleep and then a massive fire had broken out, he escaped to Turkey, but his girlfriend was being held captive until his return.

I then helped him back to Russia and aided him in the rescue of his girlfriend. It was as if I was a secret agent. The Man then gave me a black bag and told me to give it to President Putin. The dream then faded and I was then in the presence of Mr Putin, he stood before me and then said, "hand me the bag", I then handed the bag to him, he then emptied the contents onto a table revealing a Ballistic Missile, a Star Wars toy and six toy Russian agents. I then handed him a copy of my book "Five Fives Beyond Imagination". As he held it in his hand the cover slowly began to fade.

A Year later the same month, March dreams are spontaneous psychic events, messages from the subconscious a tantalizing glimpse of the future. I cannot explain why this one dream predicted so many events that have unfolded. In March 2018, I read Turkey wants to buy Russian made S-400 Triuf anti-aircraft Missiles worth billions. This has created a rift with NATO the United States has threated to impose economic sanctions on Turkey in a bid to dissuade Ankara from going ahead with the deal.

The missile out classes American weapons and can destroy Cruise Missiles and Ballistic Missiles. I then read about a fire that broke out in March 2018 in a shopping centre, the death toll was sixty-four and six bodies had not been recovered. We then have in March 2018 Sergei Skripal an ex-spy sixty-six years of age and his daughter aged thirty-three poisoned with a nerve agent at their house.

I dreamt of a black bag and six Russian Agents did they carry out this operation and why did the number six appear so many times in these events? On the 20.6.17, I lay in bed dreaming of whales washed up on a beach. I later turned on the television to discover whales had died due to plastic pollution.

On the 26.6.17, I dreamt someone was knocking on my front door. In the dream, I left my bed and answered the door stood before me was six friends from my past. All six where young once more one of them then said, "I have lost a key have you found it? The key to Eternity".

The next dream was on the 28.8.17, a visit to a different dimension. I was on a cruise ship which docked in a strange land, my departed father appeared and informed me he was to be my guide. We visited a land of green, everything was clear in a land of no fear. I gazed at a city of green I took photographs of what I had seen. The climate was hot the sun shone bright, oh such glorious golden rays of light. I walked for many miles. I addressed the many smiles; I saw the faces as if I was there, I spoke to people without a care. This was a truly amazing place could it have been Heaven?

On the 8.9.17, I dreamt I was in the sky looking down at a hurricane in America. Oh, such devastation and then calm, I watched a flock of flamingos being rehomed ahead of the hurricane the following day I turned on my computer and the first I saw was the flock of Flamingos like in my dream.

The next dream on the 15.10.17, I lay in bed a dream which kept repeating itself again and again. I could see the letter M and a white car driving, it then lost control it came off the road and then exploded in a field. The following day I turned on the computer and visited MSN. I noticed a car the same as the one in my dream that had exploded in a field after losing control. The letter M stood for Malta, a journalist by the name of Daphne Caruana Galizia who died from a car bomb just like in my dream, location Malta.

On the 2.11.17 I dreamt of rain and floods around the UK after the dream we had rain and floods. I sat writing my author's notes on the 1.4.18. I then went to bed and began to dream, I dreamt I was in an old house it was dirty and dark. I lay in bed, but it was so cold, so I got out of bed and opened a cupboard and got out some more blankets. I then noticed lots of people in the corner of the room doing a Ouija board, they were getting lots of messages of which I cannot remember. Suddenly a soldier ant appeared and came towards me from within the board I went to kill it and was then informed it couldn't die. The dream then switched to a hotel of sin it was full of evil spirits. There were lots of strange things happening I entered a lift to go to my room. I remember I could not get out until I remembered a number which was 4006, could this be a date? Maybe 4.6.18 on which an event may occur or the year after.

My predictions are numerous dream prophecy, a connection between the subjective mind and the external universe. I read that some wild- talented individuals can by inward concentration, using the right techniques actually foresee external events that have not happened yet. The occurrence of prospective dreams cannot be denied. synchronicity appears to happen at random; to be able to precipitate them at will would be almost impossible.

I remember in March 2016 builders arriving at my house to do some work. I awoke with a song playing in my head again and again the song was by Genesis entitled "That's all." The builders arrived and one of them turned on the radio and then the song I had been thinking of, came on the radio.

Another example on the 29.3.17, I watched "American Werewolf in London." The following day, I turned on the radio and the DJ played the theme tune to the movie.

I had a vision of an old episode of "Supernatural" the one in which Dean said, "I shot the sheriff, but I didn't kill the deputy." I had an urge to move my settee, I did so there was an old DVD disc. I put it in the player and to my amazement, the episode I was thinking of came on. Later I sat watching an old DVD, the best of the bangles, the hit, "Walk Like an Egyptian" came on. I watched it twice and wondered why only two people were featured doing the hand movement. One, Princess Diana who died eleven years later and colonel Gaddafi who died in 2011.

In the past, I have dreamt of famous people and then the following day I have found out they have passed away that night.

My daughter sent me a text from college, I was listening to the song "American Pie". I read the message as the song played, 'the day the music died'. It read did you know David Bowie has died? I then went out, got into my car and turned on the radio the news was on and an American said, "it was the day the music died."

I visited my mother's house; I had a bad feeling something was going to happen to me. I walked into the kitchen and then gazed into the back garden and saw my mother trying to pull out a dead plant. I had a vision of her falling backwards and without thinking, I rushed to help her and then walked into a glass door. Blood poured from a wound I eventually stopped the flow of blood, and then remembered how Numerology had played a part in all my life's events.

The date 4.2.17 added together spells B.C. which is my mother's initials. On its own the 4 is D for David, 2 is B for blood and 1 is A for accident and 7 G for garden. Philosopher Pythagoras believed numbers are the essence of life as do I.

I have been on cruises all over the world and have had lots of strange things happen to me. I remember booking a Crimea cruise because I was interested in the history regarding the charge of the light brigade, months later Russia invaded the Crimea so that destination was cancelled. I went on the cruise and docked in the morning in Romania. I woke up to explosions and went on deck. I could see fighter jets and helicopters and then out at sea a frigate firing at another boat. Then the captain apologised he went on to say he had no idea it was their national arms day.

I got off the ship and walked six miles into town to witness the military bands and their display of weapons. I visited Israel and the birthplace of Jesus; I remember buying a gold star of David necklace from a shop. Crossing the border was an absolute nightmare I sat at the front of the coach and witnessed a car full of people cross over a white line you weren't supposed to cross.

All of a sudden, Israeli soldiers appeared with lots of weapons pointed at the car screaming at the top of their voices. I remember thinking please don't open fire.

When I got back to the ship, I put on my necklace I remember going to sleep and dreaming of the necklace disappearing without a trace. I woke up and it was gone, I searched the whole cabin but to no avail.

In October 2016 I made lots of Facebook friends, one, in particular, sent me a message about angel number nine, as I had been studying numerology- 2016 nine years from my books predicted ending.

I was due to fly to Lanzarote, which is nine letters, my seat number was 33c the c represents the number three again nine. My minibus was 39. I arrived late the reception was closed so I complained and was awarded their best room, number 315 yes again number nine. I met lots of people someone said it had been raining until I arrived and that I had brought the sun with me. A couple from down South spoke with me, the lady informed me she was a gypsy, we exchanged stories she listened and then said, "You have some sort of gift from God." she then said, "Go to church and pray for answers to find out your true purpose on Earth."

I stayed for nine nights and the evening I left it poured down. I arrived at the airport and spoke to a couple of strangers. I later found out they were sitting next to me on the flight home, coincidence I had done this on three other holidays. I wonder what odds a betting man would have given me on this happening on three separate occasions.

A famous American contacted me with a message reading "you have a gift of prophecy, but you are without Jesus, you are in terrible danger, you are open to Jezebel." Another American pointed out to believe is receive and most unawakened do not look beyond the borders of their own equilibrium.

On the 9th of November 2017, I visited a shop and bought a DVD entitled "Conspiracy" the main actor was Val Kilmer. I remember rushing into Asda with a trolley that had a used coffee cup inside it, I picked it up and noticed it had my Christian name on it. I quickly did my shopping and was at the checkout when the woman in front of me struck up a conversation about "Watership Down", the movie. I mentioned the book and the haunting soundtrack Bright Eyes. Later I watched the movie in disbelief as Val Kilmer visited a Library in search of a book which he stole and ended up in jail, the book was Watership Down. Once again, the impossible.

In my first book, I mentioned the world would end in 2025 which adds to nine representing the letter I two add two is the letter D and five the letter E which spells out DIE. My predictions have a habit of becoming true so in my next book I decided to extend this date to the year 2050 the number 2 is B, the number 5 is E, add together number 7 which is G this spells out BEG.

I read about a Christian conspiracy theorist who claimed the end of the world would start on the 15th of October and end in 2024. I dreamt on the 16.10.16 the signs would start on 16.10.17 I guess I was right. I looked out my window and witnessed lots of people gazing into the sky, the sun was bright red. A hurricane had been blowing, I turned on the radio and the DJ said, "today is so spooky, no birds, darkness like something out of a Stephen King novel." Let's all hope my other prediction does not come true.

www.ingramcontent.com/pod-product-compliance
Lightning Source LLC
Chambersburg PA
CBHW022103170626
46808CB00002B/573